STEWART
and
JEAN

STEWART
and
JEAN

J. BOYETT

SALTIMBANQUE BOOKS

NEW YORK

BY THE SAME AUTHOR

The Little Mermaid (A Horror Story)

Brothel

Ricky

The Victim (and Other Short Plays)

Poisoned (a play)

For Mary Sheridan.

For my parents.

For Pam Carter, Dawn Drinkwater, and Andy Shanks.

ACKNOWLEDGMENTS

Mary Sheridan was among the early readers. Kelly Kay Griffith and Rob Widdicombe provided me with extensive notes and edits. Mary Sheridan agreed to go get drunk with me at Chevy's for "research," so thanks for that.

STEWART
and
JEAN

One

It was spring, and the Astoria beer garden was bustling, loud groups scattered in clumps among the long picnic tables, bright in the nighttime floodlights. Still, Jean and Stewart had been able to find a relatively secluded spot. The fresh breeze swept the air clean. "It's so nice," said Jean.

"Yes," said Stewart.

Jean eyed his mug. She was trying to pace herself so they would finish at the same time. "I'll get the next round," she said.

"Oh, no."

"Come on, I insist."

"No way."

He was cuter than his picture had been. That was a nice surprise. Jean stopped herself from suggesting they get a pitcher, the way she would have done with one of her girlfriends—she didn't want to risk getting drunk enough to go home with this guy.

They finished their beers. Bulldozing over her protests, he went to buy the next round himself. Although a little exasperated by his insistence, she mainly thought it was sweet.

Jean checked her e-mail on her phone and texted back a girlfriend who'd texted to ask how it was going ("good so far," she wrote), and finished in time to clink mugs with him upon his return. That first swallow of the new mug was like a pleasurable jolt of cold electricity.

"So what do you do?" she asked.

"Oh," he said, ducking his head, "I'm just kind of looking right now."

Jean got the distinct vibe he didn't want to talk about it. "Hey," she said, reassuringly, "the economy."

"Yeah, I know. Tell me about your job."

"Oh, it's boring," she said. Which it was, but as she described it she made it sound even worse. "IT stuff. Web development." The nicest part, she told him, was that she got to work across the street from Bryant Park. Obviously it was a convenient location, being right next to Grand Central. "And even though the crowds can sometimes be annoying, I actually kind of get off on all the bustle, and being right in the middle of Manhattan. I'm still a little starry-eyed about the city, I guess." The major drawback of the location, she joked, was that there was a Chipotle restaurant on the ground floor and she was always having to resist the urge to stuff her face in there.

"Although I don't know," she said. "I love New York, but I sometimes think about moving upstate. Or to Pennsylvania, even. Getting a car, commuting."

Stewart wrinkled his nose. "Why?"

"I don't know. I love New York, but I like greenery too, and I like change. Commuting would be a way to change but still stay in the city. Why live in one quasi-foreign northeastern town when you could live in two?"

It turned out Stewart had just read a book about Grand Central, so they talked some about that. He asked some intelligent questions about her job; he might be temporarily unemployed, but he was plainly smart, and even seemed to know a bit about web design. Jean was going to start asking about his background, when he said, "You're very beautiful."

Jean actually blushed, and reconsidered that pitcher. "Oh, thank you, that's so sweet." Jean was happy enough with the way she looked—wavy black hair, athletic body, big eyes—that she didn't need the affirmation, but it was still charming to hear him say so. There was something intense about Stewart. He smiled at her, he was interested in her, but there was something aloof about it, almost challenging. It would have put a lot of women off, but Jean dug it. Maybe it was perverse, but she found herself turned on by her sense that, if they were to hook up, they'd wind

4

up fighting a lot. "I was actually just thinking that you're cuter than your profile picture."

"Oh, so I have an ugly picture?"

"*No*, that's not what I meant."

"Can I make a confession? I saw your picture on OKCupid a long time before I ever messaged you."

"A long time? How long?"

"Oh. Couple weeks."

"How come you waited?"

"I guess I had to work up to it."

Jean took a long pull on her beer, still eyeing Stewart. He was laying it on pretty thick, but who cared. Once she'd swallowed, she said, "So what was it about my profile that made you message me?"

"Your photo."

"That seems shallow. What about my witty self-description? My painstakingly-assembled list of favorite books?"

"I read those. But it was the photo that made me write to you."

"Hm. I'll take that as a compliment.... You know, to be honest, I was on the fence about writing you back."

"Because of my non-cute profile picture?"

"No, and I didn't say it wasn't cute.... It was because your message was so intense. In a good way. But also in a, Whoa, way."

"You mean all that about how I'd never written to a woman on OKCupid before, but felt like I had to get in touch with you?"

"Mainly that."

"Well. It was the truth. I figured I may as well tell the truth, right?"

"Sure."

There was an awkward lull. Jean killed time with another swig, and then, when the pause kept going, she gestured at the beer garden as a whole and said, "I love this place."

"It's cool."

"So you've never been here?"

"No. I just moved to New York a week ago."

"Oh, wow! I must have been hogging the conversation and not letting you talk about yourself at *all*."

"No, no."

"Where did you move here from?"

"Arkansas."

Jean brought her mug down on the table with a thump. *"What?"*

"I'm from Arkansas."

"Oh my God." Stewart merely looked at her. "Oh my God!" She fluttered her hands, raised her voice, trying to convey the momentousness of the occasion. So far he didn't seem properly impressed. *"I'm* from Arkansas!" she finally let fly.

Even now he didn't seem blown away. In fact, he said, "I know."

"How?"

"Well, for starters, it says so on your OKCupid profile."

"Dude. Do you know the *odds* of us both being from Arkansas? I never meet anyone from home! Where are you from?"

"Conway."

"I'm from Fayetteville."

"I know."

That was right, she'd put her hometown on her profile, too. "That's amazing," she said. Stewart didn't disagree, neither did he look particularly amazed. "And, what, you just up and moved last *week*? What brought you here?"

"Just something I had to do."

"Yeah, I can understand that. I love Arkansas, but I was ready to get out of there by the time I left.... Wow, you're from Conway. I went to school there!"

"I went to school in Little Rock."

"You seem so much less amazed than I am."

Stewart shrugged apologetically.

"I mean, I lived in Conway for four years," Jean said. "What's your last name?"

"Bruno."

Jean stopped short. She stared at Stewart and tried to tell herself that Bruno wasn't such an uncommon name—but from the unconfused, challenging way Stewart met her gaze, she knew.

When he didn't volunteer anything, she said, "I knew a Bruno once."

Stewart nodded. "Kevin Bruno," he said. "But I think that was in Rogers, right? Not Conway."

The real sounds of the beer garden were distant and faint— the ringing in her ears grew loud enough to hurt. Her nerves were numbed; the knowledge of what her flesh touched, like her fingertips on the cold wet glass of the mug, all came in as superficial information emptied of sensual content. Unable to think quite clearly, she cast back through a lifetime of movie-watching, looking for some generic movie character she might channel, who could field all questions for her. "It was in Conway I met him," she said. "And knew him. Went to school with him. But I did last see him in Rogers."

"Right. Sorry."

He was still smiling. Jean looked more closely, and wondered how she could have been so blind as to have missed it before: the angrier he got, the bigger he smiled.

She started to feel something like anger herself, though the quivering massive emotion was too big, dangerous, and unstable to identify precisely. It would have been like staring at the sun in order to list all the colors it consisted of. "So you, like, what, messaged me as a joke?"

"Not a joke," he snarled. He collected himself, waited till he was back under control to continue talking. "Like I said. I saw your picture. And when I saw it, I had to write you."

"No you didn't."

"Yes I did. I had to meet you."

"For a fucking date."

"Just to meet. I mean, obviously I couldn't tell you the real reason."

"Yeah. Obviously. No shit. So you, what, you just moved out here last week, logged onto OKCupid, and spotted my profile?"

"I saw it when I was still in Arkansas." Under the circumstances, it was absurd to think either of them could manage an emotion as petty as embarrassment, but from the way Stewart dropped his eyes it was plain that was what he was feeling. "I always daydream about moving to New York. And so I set the search function on OKCupid to show me girls in New York instead of Conway because, I don't know, New York's where I liked to fantasize about living. And then when your photo popped up it was different. Then I knew I had to come."

"So I'm the one who finally motivated you to come. So you ought to be thanking me."

His face spasmed and then contorted with so much rage that Jean thought he might hit her. She forced herself to calm down, to take some deep breaths and look at it from his point of view. Not so as to sympathize, but so as to predict what he'd do next. "Okay," she said. "So. You've met me. So? Now what?"

Finally the smile was gone. Stewart was scowling and breathing deeply as he glowered at her. It seemed like he might cry. "I just wanted to see you," he managed to get out. "I wanted to at the time, but the police and everybody else told me not to. But I always regretted letting them talk me out of it, and when I happened to see your profile, I knew I wasn't going to be able to live with myself if I didn't, didn't confront you."

"Okay. Whatever. Confront me."

"You with your smart, sexy pictures, with your cutesy little description of yourself and how smart and ambitious you are. Not a care in the world and meanwhile my brother's dead."

That wild emotion Jean dared not directly look at was bubbling over. Gripping the handle of her mug like she'd go spinning off the planet otherwise, she leaned forward across the table. "I haven't a care in the world *because* your brother's dead," she hissed. "He tried to rape me. Luckily I had a gun, so I shot him in the chest. I'm sorry for your loss but I would do it again."

"Yeah, well, I don't believe my brother would ever try to rape somebody."

"Yeah, well, he did, and the police believed it too." Jean realized she was trembling, and wasn't sure her legs would work—she stood up, and found that they did. "Thanks for the beers," she said, and started to walk away, then turned back and said, "Don't follow me." She walked out of the beer garden, keeping her eyes forward, even turning her nose up a little, making herself walk in a straight line. When she passed the huge bouncer at the entrance she wouldn't allow herself to stop and talk to him, not that she knew exactly what she would have asked him for. It wasn't very late and the neighborhood was pretty crowded—she'd probably be okay. It wasn't till she was nearly a block away from the beer garden that she looked over her shoulder to make sure her date wasn't following her. All things considered, she figured she was handling this pretty well, whatever it was.

Two

The whole thing was unnerving, that was for sure. Jean called some friends back home to talk about it, once she was sure her voice wouldn't shake. Most thought she should call the police on Stewart. "For what?" she said. All he'd done was move to New York, then contact her via her publicly available dating-site profile. Maybe if he continued trying to contact her, she would try to get a restraining order or something. Not that she could really argue with her friends. Perhaps the wise thing would have been to notify the police, regardless of whether or not she thought he'd technically committed a crime. Maybe she preferred not to think about any of it.

Besides, in her most empathetic moods, she felt she could maybe understand where he was coming from. If he really did believe his brother had been innocent. In that case, she could understand how a normal, non-violent guy might have felt driven to confront her.

A few days went by. In the building where Jean worked on Forty-Second, there was a bookstore, Temple Books, next to the Chipotle. Not many bookstores left in New York, and even less in other cities, she figured. She liked to go there sometimes, during her lunch break or after work, to chill out and browse.

Today was like that. She'd brought a lunch to eat in the park, but it was past the middle of the day and she still wasn't hungry. So she decided to hang out at Temple. She got a hot chocolate in a to-go cup from their café and took it with her as she went wandering through the books. First she paused among the bestseller display tables, to see what the world was reading. Some of them, like Cormac McCarthy, she planned to get to someday. Others she gawked at with a kind of delicious, self-indulgent horror, like a series of books called *Skinny Bitch*. The cashiers and manager stood in a square enclosure, raised like a dais, presumably so they could keep an eye out for shoplifters. She'd never exchanged a word with any of them except when she was buying something, but they'd become familiar enough that she kind of felt like she knew them.

She didn't let herself get too caught up in the bestsellers, since she was only here for an hour at most and didn't have a whole idle day stretching before her. Moving through the display tables and past the Sci-Fi section, she made a right before hitting General Fiction—tucked in behind the register and before the bathroom hallway was a tightly-packed niche containing Cultural Studies. She'd thought Feminism was back here, too, but she'd misremembered—it was around the corner. Still, it was a nice quiet section, and in front of her face she saw Jacobs's *Life and Death of American Cities*, which was on her list of books to read. A moment after she'd picked it up and started thumbing through it, she was absorbed. There was a step-stool, for reaching the higher shelves. Absently Jean sat on it and turned the pages back to start the book at the beginning.

For a long time she stayed that way, alone, except for a guy in his forties whose body odor was somewhat strong and who crouched near her, reading Schopenhauer with an intense scowl. Jean didn't mind the company, or the odor. She would have liked to think his company was more suitable for her than that of most of her web design colleagues, though she didn't know if that was true. Guys who read Schopenhauer were cool.

Sipping her hot chocolate, she realized it wasn't hot anymore. That snapped her out of her absorption, since it meant she must have been here a while. She checked her phone and saw that it was indeed time to head back up to the office. Slurping down the dregs of her chocolate, she headed to the cashiers, Jacobs book in hand.

As she approached the register she wasn't paying much attention, because she was looking around for a wastebasket to throw her now-empty cup in, so she didn't actually look fully at the cashier till after she'd extended the arm holding the book. Then her fingers went flaccid and she took a step backward as the book fell to the floor. At the slapping sound it made, people turned to look.

Towering above her on the raised platform, looming over her, Stewart looked like he belonged here, in his black T-shirt and trimmed goatee. Holding his eyes on her with no special effort, he blithely said, "I saw you come in."

But if that were true he must have been somewhere other than here at the registers. Because she would have noticed him when she came in, standing here among all these guys she almost felt like she knew.

Again there was a mental hum that all but supplanted the real noise of the store around her. Again there was a strong and unstable sensation that she dared not quite look at, but this time it was more akin to fear than anger. "What are you doing here?" she whispered.

Stewart frowned and turned an ear towards her. "What?" he said, with apparent sincerity.

"What are you doing here?" she repeated, at closer to a normal volume.

"I work here," he said, as if it were obvious, which it was.

Jean took a step towards him, out of some complicated mixture of motives. Underfoot she could feel the book she'd dropped, and was dimly aware she should move back, because you weren't supposed to step on books. She had no idea what to say to him. Whatever she might say, she was afraid it would come out as a plea rather than a threat.

Suddenly there was the short, heavyset, bald Jamaican manager standing next to Stewart, pointing at her feet and saying, "Excuse me, please don't walk on the books, ma'am!"

She stepped back. She crouched down to pick up the book; the whole time she kept her eyes on Stewart, which meant that she had to fish around blindly with her hand to find the book, which probably made her look ridiculous, possibly crazy.

Stewart held her gaze, too, but he did it uncertainly, as if he weren't sure why she was reacting like this. Putting on a show for everyone else. Fucking with her. It was weird, the sense of betrayal that was mixed in with everything she was feeling. Probably because of how cute she'd thought he was when they'd first met, back when their date was going well. She remembered how excited she'd been, when it had turned out they were both from Arkansas.

She placed the book on the counter. Her voice was like a heavy bucket filled to the brim that she was carefully trying to move without spilling as she said, "This is really fucked up."

Stewart nodded and said, "Yeah," as if her observations were regrettable but true. He picked up the book. "Did you want to purchase this?"

"Fuck you," she managed to say, and walked carefully out. It was harder than it had been the other night at the beer garden.

Upstairs at her office she went into the bathroom. What she really wanted was to wash her face with cold water, but she was wearing make-up and didn't want to screw it up. Even so, she managed to cool off pretty well. Or so she thought. But she didn't last ten minutes at her computer till she had to again retreat to the ladies' room.

This time her co-worker Marissa noticed her condition. As Jean walked by her cubicle Marissa asked if she was okay, but Jean seemed not to hear. Marissa hesitated, then returned to her computer screen, where she had been trading "yo' mamma" jokes with a friend over Instant Messenger. Jean was probably just sick, like to her stomach, and wouldn't appreciate Marissa intruding. But Marissa couldn't keep her mind on her work. She knew good and well that Jean hadn't looked merely sick to her stomach— something had happened. She'd looked like someone had died, and it was sad to imagine her alone in the bathroom with whatever the bad thing was. Finally Marissa got up to go check on her, out of concern but also a bit out of nosiness and boredom.

Besides, she was always on the look-out for chances to get to know Jean better. Marissa found her co-worker fascinating.

14

She was so smart and confident and centered. Almost like she was on a higher plane or something.

Upon entering the bathroom, Marissa saw that Jean hadn't even managed to make it to a stall. Her body was a curve supported by the straight, joint-locked left arm attached to the rim of the sink, quivering with tension. Her right hand was raised to her face, her head was bowed. Approaching from behind, Marissa could see that Jean was shaking, but couldn't yet tell if she was crying, really. "Jean?" she asked, holding out her hand but not quite daring to touch Jean with it, wanting to see her face but afraid that walking around to look at it unasked would be a breach of privacy.

"Hey, Marissa," Jean answered in a raspy, shaky whisper.

This was enough of an invitation for Marissa to step around in front of Jean, look at her face, and come closer to touching her arm, though her hand still hovered an inch or two away. "What *happened*?"

Most of Jean's downturned face was hidden by her hand, but Marissa could make out something like a grimace on her mouth, and the noise she made was almost like a disbelieving laugh. She shook her head, and said, "You wouldn't believe me."

"Of course I will. Come on, tell me what's wrong."

Jean took in and released a few more shuddery breaths. "There's a guy in the bookstore downstairs."

Then it seemed like she would quit talking. "Yeah?" prompted Marissa. A guy in the bookstore downstairs? What was the worst he could have done, flash her? That didn't seem like such a big deal.

Still in that shaky voice, still with her face hidden, Jean said, "We're both from the same place."

Marissa tried to recall Jean's talk about home. "Kentucky?" she hazarded.

"No. Arkansas."

"Okay."

Marissa waited. It started to seem like Jean wasn't going to volunteer anything more. Could it be some Southern thing?

Although she was starting to suspect Jean just plain didn't want to talk about it, she couldn't help but prod her once more: "And, so, I mean, did he do something?"

"No. I did." Jean shrugged, and sighed, and shook her head as if it were just one of those things, and said, "I shot his brother."

"What?"

"I shot his brother."

"Like, with what?"

"I shot him in the chest with a gun and killed him. This was in Rogers. Rogers, Arkansas. That's not far from Fayetteville. We were at some friends' house, but the friends weren't there. Me and him had been flirting, I guess. He tried to rape me, so I grabbed the gun and I shot him."

Marissa gaped at her. "Oh. My. *God*."

Jean's trembling intensified, and a tear slid down her chin out from behind her hand. "And I don't feel fucking bad about it," she said, her voice thicker.

"Oh my God," Marissa said again, then, rallying herself, "No, of course you shouldn't. You have a right to *defend* yourself!" Privately, she was reeling. It was one thing to know that Jean hailed from gun country. It was another to hear she'd killed somebody with one, regardless of the circumstances. And apparently without much legal fuss.

Soon she was able to blink past the after-image of the revelation, and return to the issue at hand: "You said this guy's *brother* was in the bookstore downstairs?"

"Yes."

"What, he just happens to be in town?"

"He moved to New York. He fucking works down there now. I guess he's stalking me." And she recounted to Marissa how she'd met Stewart; how he'd supposedly been looking on OKCupid for New York girls, and happened to see her picture; how that apparently had been motive enough for him to move up here; how he'd sent her this charming albeit intense message on OKCupid, and after going back and forth about it she'd written back and agreed to meet; how they'd been having

16

actually a pretty nice date, when Stewart had sprung his trap on her.

"Jesus," Marissa said. One of the oddest parts of the story, to her, was the notion of some guy in Arkansas idly scrolling through the dating profiles of girls a thousand miles away in New York. Why? Because he couldn't jerk off without fantasizing he was boning someone in a big city?

"What are you going to do?" asked Marissa.

"I don't know," Jean said. She still had not quite lost control, though her voice was slightly wobblier and tears were still leaking out from behind her hand. "I mean, I guess he's just going to be *down* there now."

It was true that Marissa had been in part distracted from her compassion by the fact that this was some of the juiciest gossip she'd ever heard. But now she began to realize the horror of Jean's situation. "No," she said firmly. "No, he can't do that."

"It's not illegal to work there."

"We'll explain to the owner and make him fire the guy."

Jean shrugged dubiously.

By now, Marissa had touched Jean. Her hand squeezing the other woman's shoulder, she said, "Anyway, for right now the important thing is that we need to get you out of here. Just say you're sick and go home, I'll cover for you." A thought struck her. "How did this guy know you worked here?"

"I told him, like an idiot. During our date."

"You're not an idiot, don't call yourself that. But you didn't tell him where you live, did you? Like, your address, or exact train stop?"

"No." Jean paused. She seemed calmer, trembled less; Marissa thought that this concrete question, scary as it might be, was distracting Jean somewhat from her plight. "I don't remember doing that. I'm sure I wouldn't have. I mean, he knows I live in Astoria. He could tell that from my OKCupid profile."

"Right. Well, listen, I don't mean to freak you out, but you need to make sure he doesn't follow you home. Like, wait for you to come out of the building and trail you without your noticing."

"Right." Again, the introduction of a practical consideration seemed to have a calming effect. Jean's voice was steadier, and she even let her hand fall from her face to reveal her damaged makeup. However, she still didn't look directly at Marissa as she said, "But, I mean, I'd never know for sure if he wasn't trailing me, or if I just didn't notice him."

"For today at least you don't have to worry about that. After you leave I'll go downstairs and make sure he's still there in the store. If it turns out he did disappear around the same time you left, then I'll call and warn you and we'll figure something out."

Jean agreed to the plan. Marissa escorted her down to hail a taxi. Marissa told everyone that it was convenient for her to accompany Jean, since she hadn't taken her lunch break yet and could go ahead and do that now.

Marissa put Jean in a cab and watched till it was safely out of sight. Then she turned to face Temple Books.

She went in and scanned the interior. She didn't love hanging out in bookstores as much as Jean did, but she'd been in here several times and the place was more or less familiar, and as she scanned the employees behind the register she recognized most of them. There was the Jamaican in the purple knit shirt, who she thought was a manager. There was a guy in a tweed jacket and a bow tie, even though he was only like forty—he was kind of cool-looking, actually. The third guy behind the register had to be this Stewart person. He wore a black T-shirt and had a neatly-trimmed goatee, just like Jean had described him.

Marissa pretended to be browsing through the bestseller tables as she eyed the guy. Jean had also called him cute, but Marissa didn't see that at all. Sure, his haircut was fine and he wasn't fat or anything. But his eyes were too big, almost buggy, and you could tell from his face he'd have jowls one day.

He glanced at her, then away, then again glanced at her and looked away, then finally held eye contact and raised his shoulders and jutted his head at her with a "what?!" gesture. It affronted Marissa that he would have the gall to even return her gaze, considering the shit he was pulling. She marched up to his register, tilting her head back so she could look up at him, and demanded, "Excuse me, but are you looking at me?"

"You were looking at me, ma'am," he said, as if she were crazy.

"That's right, you were, Miss," said the Jamaican manager, whom she'd totally forgotten about even though he'd been standing right next to Stewart the whole time.

"This is between me and him," said Marissa. Which actually wasn't true, it was between him and Jean, but that didn't occur to her right now.

"So handle it after he gets off work, please," said the manager.

"I've never even seen this girl before," the guy Stewart told his boss.

That was true, he had no way of knowing who she was. But, again, his whole scheme struck her as so egregious that it seemed he simply had to know what she was mad about; if someone walked to him and was angry, surely he had to say to himself, *Maybe they're angry about the shitty thing I'm doing.* So it was with outrage at his dishonesty that she said, "You know good and well why I'm here."

"Not really," he said. Before she could lash out at him, he added, "Are you friends with Jean or something?," thereby proving her point, that he'd known all along what she was riled about.

"Yes," she said. "What makes you think you can come around and harass people?"

"I'm not harassing anybody. I'm just working here."

"What is she talking about?" asked the manager. "Harassing who?"

"That girl from earlier," Stewart told him, "the one who stepped on the book."

That was all the manager needed to hear: "All right, ma'am, I think this is something you and Stewart can discuss after his shift."

"Don't you want to know what kind of person you've got working here?"

"Not especially."

19

Before she could retort, Stewart cut her off. Glaring at her, he demanded, "*I'd* like to know. What kind of person?" His voice had risen along with hers and people were watching them now. Customers who had been hidden among the shelves were wandering to the front of the store to see what was going on. "Huh? What kind? Tell us, what kind?"

It was on the tip of Marissa's tongue to reply, "A rapist." She was glad she stopped herself, because of course that wasn't true. He was the brother of a rapist, but that wasn't at all the same thing. She nearly started talking loudly about what he was doing, harassing Jean with his mere presence if nothing else, but explaining it might be tricky—she didn't want to sound like she was mad at him because his brother had been shot. Moreover, she'd have to reveal that Jean had shot a guy, and since that was private information she ought to consult her friend first.

Which meant she was stuck, seething under his glare, unable to respond to it. What with the righteous anger painted over his face, anyone casually watching would have thought he was the wronged party, he played it so well.

"You know good and well," was all she said.

He said, "Anything I know, I'm not afraid for you to say in front of these people."

"Yeah, well." The realization of how little she could say had not only galled her, it had also put her in a state of high anxiety as she tried to figure out how she was going to extricate herself from this scene with dignity. The options were limited. Finally, she said, "We'll be watching you," which she knew sounded stupid even as she said it, and she spun on her heel to leave.

Behind her, Stewart called, "Thanks, ma'am, be sure to come again."

Three

Dan, the owner, had heard the commotion from his office, and apparently having no stronger distraction at the moment called Stewart up there to interrogate him.

This was Stewart's first time in the office since he'd been hired three days ago, the day after his date with Jean. It was fairly organized but not exactly neat: it was too lived-in for that, constantly in the middle of being used by a busy man.

Stewart found Dan kind of intimidating. With his big unblinking eyes, his grizzled graying beard, his wiry short frame taut in his jogging shorts with T-shirt tucked in, he struck Stewart as a real New Yorker.

"So what the hell was all that down there?" demanded Dan.

Still fresh off the bus from Arkansas, Stewart felt from Dan's tone that they were on the verge of a fistfight. "I never saw that girl before," he said, maintaining an appearance of calm.

Dan turned his head so that he was looking at Stewart out of the corners of his eyes, wary of this obvious bullshit. "So you have no idea who that girl was? She just came in here out of the blue and started yelling at you, and you didn't do anything at all to provoke it?"

"I never saw her before, but she's friends with a girl I know."

"Well, how do you know this other girl?"

That was a complicated question. But Dan was losing patience, so Stewart said, "We went on a date." It was kind of a lie, but at least it was true.

Like Stewart had flipped a switch, Dan sat back and said "Oh." He relaxed into his chair, all of a sudden twenty percent less intense. He nodded. "Gotcha."

"It wasn't, like, a serious thing...."

"Hey, hey, I understand. Women. Only, try not to bring your personal business around the store. Okay?"

"Sure. But, I mean, if she does come by again, I can't really stop her...."

"Hey, Stewart, I told you—I understand. Just do your best, all right? That's all anybody can do."

As he sent him back down onto the floor, Dan clapped him on the shoulder. Stewart almost felt like he was going to get a promotion.

Back downstairs, Stewart retook his place at the register. Peter, the manager, looked at him curiously, but when Stewart's shrug indicated he wasn't interested in discussing it, Peter nodded and asked him to go out on the floor and do some shelving.

Charles was shelving too, somewhat lackadaisically, and he let himself go almost into a trance as he watched Stewart. Charles had been hired only the week before, and so took an interest in his fellow newbie. Plus Stewart was from Arkansas. On the one hand, that seemed moderately exotic; on the other hand, Charles himself was from Spokane, which was not exactly cosmopolitan, either. And though he'd been in New York nearly two and a half years he still felt like a new arrival.

Even though there were still books on the cart he'd been assigned, Charles went to help Stewart with his. He timed it so that he and Stewart stepped up to the cart at the same moment. "Hey," he said.

Stewart barely glanced at him, a look that suggested it was weird for Charles to be talking to him when they had all this work. "Hey," he said, and walked off with a stack of books, not pausing to chat.

Charles worked on his own cart until he was able to again time a simultaneous arrival at Stewart's. "So," he said quickly, before Stewart could escape, "can I ask you something? What was all that, earlier? With that girl?"

"Just some crazy person."

"Really? I mean, do you know her, or...?"

"Listen, I don't want Dan to come out and see me yakking on the clock, what with me being new and having been involved in that big scene earlier."

"Oh, sure, sure. I mean, I'm new, too, so...."

They each went back to working on their own carts. Even though Stewart's was more difficult—there were fewer copies of each book, and books from all over the store, which meant he had to run all over and hunt for the right spot on the shelf, whereas all Charles's books were from General Fiction and, while he had about the same number of volumes, he had only about half as many titles—despite that, Stewart finished and went back to refill his cart well before Charles. That made Charles slightly uneasy. He'd been telling himself it was okay that he was slower than everyone else, since he was still new, but Stewart was a week newer than him. Of course, there had been those few minutes when Charles had been helping with Stewart's cart, instead of doing his own.

It was too bad that skinny girl was supposedly crazy, because she'd also been hot, with her complicated red hair and big green eyes and smart black suit. Given the apparent relationship between her and Stewart, it seemed unlikely that Stewart would introduce them.

The next day Jean didn't come to work. She and Marissa had never hung out before, but when she'd left the other day she'd given Marissa her number, so Marissa could call and warn her if Stewart left the store at the same time. Marissa debated with herself whether or not to call her to check if she was all right, but regretfully concluded that they didn't know each other well enough for it to be her business.

She decided to take her mind off that drama. There would be time to talk about it later, if Jean wanted. Anyway, work was busy. By the time lunch rolled around, she was ready for a break.

In sunny Bryant Park she sat munching her salad and watching about a hundred people doing the free yoga class in the central field. It was a beginner's class. In the back few rows there were some hopeless cases. There was a fat girl attempting a downward-dog, who looked like a bowling ball trying to fold itself.

She became aware of a guy's approach. Scruffy but reasonable hair, a blue *Great Gatsby* T-shirt, tan cargo pants. Not uncute. He was approaching her cautiously, as if he didn't want to scare her off, and with some definite intention.

"Hi," he said.

"Hello," she said.

"Do you mind if I talk to you a minute?"

"Sorry, I don't want to, uh...."

"No, I just, um.... I mean, it's totally none of my business, but it's just, I know Stewart, and, uh … I guess I'm just curious."

Marissa frowned. "Stewart?"

"The guy at Temple. Who you yelled at."

"Oh." She thought back. "I don't think I *yelled* at him."

"No, well, I mean, you know."

Marissa eyed the guy with a hint of disapproval. "And so you're friends with him?"

"No, not really." Inside, Charles laughed wryly and silently at himself—he would betray any man for even the hint of the ghost of the dream of the chance for pussy. "I mean, I don't know any reason *not* to be friends with him, yet. I only met him a couple days ago."

Marissa finally realized that the guy was not here to defend Stewart, but to get the dirt on him. Bursting as she was to talk about it, she all but rubbed her palms together as she launched into the story. Charles nearly asked if he could sit with her, but stopped himself and simply sat at the table as if his right to do so were a given; that was a tip from *Secrets of the Pick-Up Artist*, which they'd been flipping through the other day at Temple. Though they'd been going through it as a joke and laughing at it, every once in a while it gave advice that seemed not bad.

The thing with Stewart and Jean was kind of an amazing story. Rather, Marissa didn't know enough to make it a story, really—it was more like a fascinating accusation. When she was done, Charles said, "Oh my God." He let it sink in a moment, then said, "So, you really think that's why he moved to New York?"

"Why else?"

Charles thought of Spokane. "Well, there are lots of reasons someone might want to leave home and move to New York."

"But then to sneak his way into a date with the girl his brother tried to rape?! And to just happen to get a job in the same building as her, out of the thousands of places to work in New York?!"

"Yeah, that is pretty fucked up." Charles paused, thinking over his next words, not wanting to give the impression of being on a different side of the conflict than her, but not yet ready to completely subscribe to the view that Stewart was a psychopath. "But, you know," he finally began, slowly, and apologetically, "she did kill his brother. I'm not trying to say she shouldn't've, or that that excuses Stewart. All I'm saying is, you know, he maybe has some issues to work through that are legitimate."

"Yes," conceded Marissa, hiding the uneasiness she felt at having blabbed Jean's secret. "But either way, I don't think it's exactly good for Jean that he's here, you know?"

"Oh, no, of course not."

"Even if he does have legitimate cause to feel upset, Jean's still the real victim."

"Totally. All I meant was, maybe he would listen to reason, if someone explained it to him the right way, made him understand what he's doing and just how, you know, inappropriate it is." His eyebrows drew together and his mouth twisted up as he uttered a phrase made ridiculous by its inclusion in a hundred thousand movies: "Do you think he's after, like, revenge?"

"I don't know," Marissa said, her eyes misty, as if transported to another realm by the sound of that non-quotidian word. "Maybe."

Charles squinted into empty space, distracted from the hot girl he was talking to. Was Stewart going to do something to Jean? Inflict violence upon her? On the one hand, that was definitely a paranoid notion. On the other other hand, this was definitely the kind of thing people did commit violence over. And getting a job in her building and taking her out on a date was plainly a form of passive, psychological violence. If he really was going to be indefinitely lurking beneath her office, how could she do anything but quit? Who could tough *that* out? But what guarantee was there he wouldn't find some perfectly good reason to be near her next job? Or apartment? Or both? "I mean, there's no way to call the cops on him, is there?"

"It seems like there should be, but when I think it over I don't see how."

Charles was relieved, because his own question had thrown him into a mild, quasi-panic. It all sounded very fucked up, but he still would hate to casually get the guy arrested. "Well, I'll talk to him."

"Yeah? About this?"

"I don't know yet. I'll feel it out. Discreetly—I won't tell him about this talk we just had. It'll be kind of natural for me to strike up conversations with him, since we're both newbies at Temple."

"Oh, yeah?"

She said it with enough genuine interest that Charles was able to finally divert the conversation from Stewart to himself. He told her how he was from Spokane, how he'd moved here to get his MFA in Creative Writing from Sarah Lawrence. "Oh, you're a writer!" she exclaimed. He modestly confirmed that he was. "That's cool," she said. She asked where he'd done his undergrad—Spokane, he told her—she asked if he'd gone to Sarah Lawrence right after getting his BA—nah, he'd futzed around a while first, wandering around Spokane trying to figure out how to get out of there. Now, he joked, he was just waiting to become rich and famous so he could pay off his student loans. She said she was sure he would, and asked if he was working on anything now. He told her he was, though it was still in the "planning phase."

Even after she'd finished her salad she lingered, chatting with him. She listened to his stories with interest and laughed a few times. She offered stories of her own, without Charles having to work hard at drawing her out.

Eventually Marissa said she needed to get back to work. Charles considered asking for her number, but decided against it. He had to check within himself and make sure his hesitation wasn't mere cowardice; if he'd decided it was, he would have forced himself to go ahead and ask. But no, it really did feel premature, even though she was smiling at him with apparent sincerity. Besides, it wasn't as if he was unlikely to bump into her again. In fact, she even said, "Well, see you in the park again, I hope."

It was time for Charles to be getting back to work, too. There was a food kiosk on the other side of the park, called Sandwichcraft. That was where Charles had been heading when he'd gotten side-tracked. It was too late now. He'd sacrificed his chance to eat, in order to talk to the hot girl.

Four

Charles left the store at five, but Stewart was on the closing shift. Temple locked its doors at nine, then they managed to get out of there before half-past. Some of the guys were going for some beers a couple blocks away, and they invited Stewart. He declined. He did think about accepting, though.

Now, in the dark, it was his turn to go to Bryant Park. He still worried about being out in a park after dark, as if he might be mugged and murdered, as if it were the Bryant Park of the seventies. This, despite the fact that there were still plenty of pedestrians and cars out. Stewart knew he was being dumb, but still thought he was doing well, considering the only big city he'd ever really spent time in was Dallas; and in Dallas, you really could get shot in the street. But Stewart had gone online and checked the stats, and knew that central Manhattan really was bizarrely safe.

The reason he wandered into the park was that he needed to make a phone call to his mother, and he didn't want to do it at home. Or where he lived, anyway—"home" seemed an odd word to apply to that apartment in Ridgewood, so far out in Queens that he still got lost trying to get to it, filled with strangers, the roommates whose Craigslist ad he'd answered while still in Arkansas. If he were to try to talk on the phone there, everyone who happened to be in the apartment would hear every word of it—he didn't even have a door he could close, he slept on a couch in the living room.

So his reason for ducking into the still-somewhat-scary park was to make a phone call; but he found himself dreading that conversation more than any of the most intimidating (and simultaneously alluring) scenes the city had to offer. He put the call off and strolled through the park, looking at the people, trying to eavesdrop.

There were so many different kinds of people. Languages he'd never heard spoken, races he couldn't identify. With a few overheard conversations, he wondered why they were privately role-playing with each other, till he realized a millisecond later that, no, they really were rich, or in the fashion industry, or whatever. He heard one woman talking and he wondered with alarm what might be wrong with her, till he realized she was simply speaking Chinese or something.

There was a fountain. He sat on its edge. Even in a crowd, there was something mystical and removed about a fountain at night.

It wasn't like he couldn't appreciate what his mother must be going through. She'd never gotten over Kevin's death six years ago. And she'd never stopped being freaked out by Stewart's suicide attempt two years after that, even though he'd explained to her multiple times that he'd never really, truly meant to go through with it. The proof was that he'd never tried a second time, right?

He took the phone out of his pocket and held it in his hand. Rubbing it, looking at it. He imagined it popping out of his hand like a soap bar he'd squeezed and landing in the fountain, thus granting him a reprieve. It didn't pop out of his hand, though. Finally he pulled up his list of contacts, pressed "Home," and held the phone to his ear as the ringing tones started.

After the third ring, he began to hope maybe no one would pick up. He had just enough time to start feeling guilty for the hope before his mother answered.

She was worried about him, but for some reason her worry first expressed itself in questions about the weather. She was very worried New York was having a heat wave. He assured her several times that, though it was hot, it was still five degrees or so cooler than it had been in Arkansas.

"Yes," she said, "but someone was telling me that it's even worse up there, because there's more concrete and it bounces the sun rays right back up into your face."

She wanted to know if that job he'd found was working out okay. He told her it was. "Well, that really was some good work on your part, finding a job straight off like that," she said. It sounded like begrudging praise—but why shouldn't it be? She'd made no secret of not wanting him to move to New York out of the blue like he had.

She wanted to hear about the apartment. He tried to keep the details from her, but soon the only way to keep her from knowing that he didn't have his very own room would have been to lie to her, and it didn't seem worth doing that. Though if he'd known in advance how horrified she'd be, he might have changed his mind.

"Do you want me to send you some money?!" she moaned.

"*No*, Mom. Just relax, it's only for right now at the beginning. Lots of people live this way when they're just starting off in the city."

Then they were quiet for a while. He felt ashamed for having spoken harshly to her. Especially since he knew good and well why it freaked her out for him to be gone.... Gentle as the sound of the fountain was, its genuine presence was almost enough to drown out her distant, tinny voice. He couldn't help but track the drifting passersby with his eyes, try as he might to concentrate on his mother half the continent away.

"Well," she said, for something to say.

Stewart had an urge to put his hand in the fountain water, but no one else was doing it. Maybe that was prohibited, or maybe the water was dirty. "So," he said. "How's Dad?"

"He's all right," she said, sounding annoyed, as if Stewart knew perfectly well that he wasn't. "He's asleep right now, or I'd put him on."

"Oh, that's too bad," he said, relieved.

There in the brightly-illuminated nighttime city he sat at the fountain and watched the crowds of busy strangers. He thought of his parents, alone in Arkansas, all alone there now that their only surviving son was gone.

Stewart had resolved to stay on the phone until he felt his duty had been done, but it still felt undone when he got off—he just couldn't bear to stay on any longer. They said goodbye, they said they loved each other, then they hung up.

He sat alone and watched the milling crowd with no idea how to mingle in it.

The next day Charles worked the early shift again, from nine to five, and again Stewart worked from noon to nine. When Stewart arrived Charles said hello and tried to strike up a conversation. He tried to be friendly enough to maintain the exchange and learn about the guy, but he was inhibited from being *too* friendly by all the stuff he'd heard about him. The conversation didn't get off the ground.

On his lunch break Charles went back to Bryant Park. He walked across to Sandwichcraft, even though it was a little pricey for him. Once he had his sandwich he sat near the spot where he'd met Marissa the day before, and idly scanned the park as he ate. He didn't see her. It was just as well. Ideally, when they met again, he should have something to tell her about that subject that interested her so much.

Five

Jean called out the day after seeing Stewart downstairs at Temple, and the next morning she was tempted to do so again. But that was crazy. What was she going to do, quit her job? It was absurd to have shot Kevin and moved to New York and still be intimidated by the incident. In comparison to those two steps, taking a bunch of sick days seemed pathetically ineffective.

At the office she made a point of smiling at everyone and saying hello and being especially cheerful. To polite inquiries after her health, she responded with a wave of her hand and the assurance that it had been nothing. In public Marissa got the same sort of greeting as everyone else, which hurt her feelings some. But when she poked her head into Jean's cubicle and asked again how she was doing, Jean granted her a wry shrug.

Something about the way Marissa's eyes seemed so carefully loaded with concern, about her hushed and serious tone, worried Jean. She saw that Marissa wanted to talk about this stuff. Jean didn't feel particularly like talking about it anymore, but she sensed that if Marissa couldn't converse about it with her, she'd find someone else.

She hadn't even told her roommate, Helen, even though Helen was one of her closest friends in the city and could tell something was bugging Jean. But if Helen found out about her weird quasi-stalker, she might start to worry, considering that she and Jean lived together. And it would be a bit much, dealing with Helen's worry and with the Stewart thing itself, both at the same time.

Anyway, for the moment, she wasn't up for either pandering to or policing Marissa.

Although her attention wandered, she managed to work competently all morning. No one watching her would have known she was disturbed—at worst they would have thought she was bored and daydreaming. Marissa was proud of her for that.

Jean decided to go to Temple at lunch. Before she'd gotten to work this morning, in fact over the last couple days, she'd simply accepted that she was going to sacrifice the store. But now that she was here she understood that was unacceptable.

The weird thing, the thing that she wondered at now, was that she had ever been scared of him. Outraged was one thing. But what could he do to her? It wasn't like she'd ever consent to be alone with him. And she carried pepper spray, so there was that if he ever tried to follow her. Fuck him.

She waited till late to take her lunch. She interrogated herself carefully as to whether or not she was putting it off out of fear, but was confident she was not. On the contrary; she *wanted* to see him.

Her timing was good. When she walked into Temple, Stewart was shelving books in the Classics section, right at the edge between it and the Bestsellers. He saw her come in. As she took her first few steps into the store, she let her eyes rest calmly on his, thick disdain soaking her mouth and drawing its corners down. Then she stopped among the islands of book-stacked tables, ostentatiously flipping through the new Cormac McCarthy hardcover.

She was aware that Stewart seemed unable to look away from her. In her peripheral vision she could see him staring at her with amazed fury, the muscles of his jaw and mouth bunching up, his eyes popping.

No doubt he had fantasized about this as some sort of old-fashioned vendetta. Back in Arkansas it had maybe seemed exotic and daring. Let him see now that actually he was nothing but a nobody working in a dead-end retail store for probably minimum wage. He was nothing to worry about.

It occurred to her that even though he worked here, he probably couldn't afford to buy one of these books. Some of these hardbacks were thirty bucks. With sales tax, that probably came out to nearly half his daily take-home; even if he were full-time, he couldn't be making much more than four hundred a week before taxes. But she could buy them. Though she wasn't rich, she still made more than seventy thousand a year. She picked up the McCarthy book and rested it in the crook of her arm, then set on top of it a hardback of the new Claire Messud novel, which she had a vague interest in. Idly she scanned the table for something else to buy. Flaunting her economic power was petty. But it was a real power, and it felt good to have a weapon, since he'd started the fight.

He was still looking at her. Slowly she let her eyes slide up from the book covers and again meet his. She kept her mouth and eyelids heavy but otherwise tried to stay expressionless. He was standing still, glaring at her, breathing hard. After a moment she let her eyes glide back down again. Not as if she were scared to hold his gaze, but as if the books were more interesting.

Even as he advanced on her, she wouldn't look up. Only when he was right at her shoulder did she raise her eyes, giving him the kind of look a fashion magnate might give to a waiter who'd sat uninvited at her table.

Seeing that he really was shaking, as if having trouble containing himself, she grew scared. But she refused to show it. Anyway, if he hit her here in the store, that would be the best thing that could happen. He'd be fired and so would no longer work in the building, and she'd be able to get a restraining order. "Yes?" she said, like speaking to him was a big concession.

"Sorry, but what was that look you gave me a second ago?"

"I noticed you were staring at me, so I glanced up to see if there was some problem."

"Uh-huh. Well, I didn't like the way you were looking at me."

"Well, I'll be more than happy not to look at you again."

They were in full view of the cashiers, and while they weren't raising their voices, they also weren't whispering. That Jamaican manager appeared beside them; "I'm sorry, is something wrong?" he asked.

"Not with me," Jean said smoothly. It would be inexact to say she was enjoying this, but she did feel exalted. This was a fight, and she was winning.

The manager might have been predisposed to be on Stewart's side—he'd always struck Jean as a guy who would rather defend his subordinates than kowtow to the customers, plus he was probably still mad that she'd stepped on that book—but Stewart looked so irrationally furious that it must have given him pause. "She was giving me dirty looks," Stewart said.

The manager turned from one to the other of them. "If you two have some personal business...."

"I'm just here on my lunch break to buy some books," Jean said, holding up the hardbacks in her arms as proof. "Your employee was staring at me. I looked back at him, but then decided to look away because it seemed silly to make a big thing out of it. That's when he came over and started talking to me."

"Well, obviously that's not all that happened. You two have some sort of personal history, and I...."

"Oh, I never said that was *all* that happened. I meant that was all that happened *today*. Stewart and I do have a history, yes. Definitely. You can ask him about it. Go ahead, I don't care. You can ask him right now."

The manager looked at Stewart, curious, waiting. But when Stewart not only failed to volunteer anything, but even dropped his eyes in shamed confusion, the manager said, "I don't care about whatever goes on between you, I just can't have it disrupting the store."

"That's fine. I just got done telling him, I'm happy to pretend he isn't here. I know I reacted like it was a big deal the other day, but it was because I was surprised. That's over, though."

Peter took Stewart aside, leaving Jean to browse. He took him to the relatively quiet hall that led to the bathrooms. He didn't want to snoop in Stewart's private business, he reiterated, but Stewart was going to have to keep his cool. Stewart nodded. Peter asked if he wanted to go ahead and take his dinner break early, but Stewart said he wasn't hungry. Peter told him to keep shelving then, but to get a new cart out of Receiving, one loaded with books for sections towards the back of the store, away from Bestsellers.

Charles had been working one of the registers and had watched the confrontation between Jean and Stewart, then Peter's intervention; though he hadn't caught every single word, he'd followed the gist. What few convictions he'd had about the situation had faltered. That Jean woman sure hadn't seemed to think she had any reason to be scared of Stewart. And Stewart had walked right up to her like he didn't have anything to hide— he didn't seem like someone who was doing something sneaky.

Jean browsed a while through the bestsellers, then wandered away.

Stewart was stocking children's books, sweating and trembling, burning up, blood pounding hard enough to cause a headache. Next to the Children's section was the Humor. Jean came drifting around the corner—quietly, but it was like an explosion in the mind. She looked at him, in the eyes, long enough to let him see she knew he was there and she wasn't startled at the sight of him. Then she just stood there, not three feet away from him, and pulled a big *Far Side* collection off the shelf and began reading. It was awkward for her to hold it, since she already had almost two hundred dollars' worth of books in her arms.

Stewart saw black spots and had trouble breathing. "You have to stand right there?" he demanded in a murmur.

She looked up at him with dead eyes. "I'm thinking of buying this book," she said.

"Looks like you already have enough books to keep you busy."

"I can afford them."

"All of a sudden you have this big urge to read *The Far Side*? When I just happen to be standing right here?"

Jean returned her attention to the book. "Hey. You were the one who came up here looking for me. Remember?"

He had to look away, seething. She was right, technically. But it was indecent, her following him around like this. It made sense for *him* to confront *her*—she was the one who'd killed his brother.

He tried to get back to shelving. The titles swam before his eyes, and he realized he was slamming the books into the shelves so hard that he was bending their covers. He forced himself to calm down. Without looking at Jean, he said, "So you're just going to keep coming around? Bugging me?"

"I'm going to come here sometimes to do some shopping, like I always have." Then she paused and looked up at him, as if the weirdness of the situation was hitting her anew. "I mean, isn't that kind of what you want? You came up here looking for me, didn't you? You saw my picture on OKCupid and decided to move to New York. You found out where I work and decided to get a job in the same building."

Stewart continued to work and seethe. What was happening now bore only the most perverse relation to what he'd had in mind, so that he could only think Jean was mocking him. Then again, he wasn't sure what he *had* expected, what he'd intended to do.

Jean watched him openly, taking in his confusion. Her eyes narrowed; he had the feeling she was realizing he wasn't a threat after all, and that the revelation inspired no sympathy in her.

He kept enough control of himself to finish shelving the children's books properly, though he did get palm sweat on some of the covers. Jean didn't look at him anymore, but she did keep standing there reading *The Far Side* till after he'd taken the empty cart away.

She was so glad to find that he didn't scare her, to find that *he* seemed to be the one who was scared, that she might have continued to lurk a while longer. But her work had piled up thanks to her sick day, so it wouldn't be a good idea to stretch her lunch hour out any more.

She left at about two-thirty. A little after three Stewart went to Peter and said he was sick and needed to go home. Peter looked dubious, but told him to go ahead. Charles was disappointed, since he'd been trying to think up ways to feel Stewart out about everything.

Charles left work at five and went across the street to the park again. To read his book, to check out girls, to look for Marissa. He had no special reason to go home. He lived in Harlem with two roommates, one of whom played video games with the volume up full blast. It dominated the whole common area. Four nights a week the guy worked as a bouncer, so it was usually no big deal. Tonight he was off.

Scanning the metal tables along the side of the park, Charles was surprised to glimpse Stewart, brooding in the sun. He wasn't even very far from the entrance of Temple—anyone walking by the park could see him if they happened to glance in the right place. After a hesitation, Charles walked over to his table.

Even once Charles was standing at his elbow, Stewart didn't look at him. It was weird. Did he really not notice him? It made Charles nervous. It brought him back to elementary school, where kids would always pick on him, and where he often didn't understand the joke. "Hey, Stewart," he said casually.

By the way Stewart wasn't startled to hear his name, you could tell that he had in fact known Charles was there and had just been ignoring him. He took a deep breath, not quite a sigh, and, not looking up at Charles but turning his head Charles's way, said with a tired voice, "Hey, man."

"You care if I sit down?" asked Charles, afraid Stewart was going to tell him to fuck off. But instead Stewart nodded and said to go ahead. Charles sat.

For nearly a minute Charles sat with him quietly, watching Stewart stare at the crowd. Finally, he said, "Hey, you know, maybe it's not a good idea to be sitting right out here where Peter or Dan can see you. Especially Dan, I think."

Stewart didn't respond.

Charles said, "Because you said you were going home sick, I mean. I mean, not that they're hard-asses or anything. But, you know. It is your first week, and all." Charles waited, to give

Stewart a chance to reply. Then he said, "And I think you said you only just moved to the city. Right? And only just found an apartment and everything. It would suck if you had to go looking for a new job and everything. I mean, not that they're going to fire you or anything. But, you know."

A moment went by. Charles got the strong impression Stewart didn't want to be talking about all this. Stewart said, "Yeah, well, you know."

Charles glanced around at all the strangers, at the girls in the skimpy summer dresses. "So," he said. "You know. You just moved here last week, right? So what brought you up here?"

Another pause. Charles wished he hadn't sat down. Stewart obviously didn't want him here. It would be weird to just stand up and walk off, but it would be even more awkward for them both to sit there in silence.

But now Stewart said, "Well. You know that girl, that I kind of got into it with today?"

"Yeah."

"Well. This is going to sound crazy, but she killed my big brother Kevin."

There was a white-noise roaring everywhere, like the whole world was inside a conch shell. This was exactly what he'd been hoping for, Charles realized now that it was here: the surreal irreality of reality itself, the privileged sphere of reality. He'd expected he would have to sneak around and ask clever questions in order to trick Stewart into revealing his secret. It was disarming to have Stewart be so frank about it, and Charles was about as tongue-tied as he would have been if it really had been a total surprise.

Even when he was able to speak, all he managed was, "She killed your brother?"

"Yeah."

"How?"

"She shot him a couple times in the chest."

"Why?"

"No good reason."

Charles thought about pursuing this the way he'd originally planned, under-handedly playing dumb with questions like, "Then how come she's not in jail?" After thinking it over, though, he said, "Hey, man. I feel like I should tell you that I actually, like, know about this stuff."

Now Stewart looked directly at him with interest. Charles explained about how he'd bumped into Marissa the other day and hadn't been able to refrain from asking her why she'd had it in for Stewart, and he told the story as Marissa had told it.

"My brother did *not* rape her," was the first thing Stewart said, angrily, when Charles was done.

"Marissa actually didn't say he had, she only said he'd tried to."

"He didn't do that either! He would never have done that, to anybody. And he *knew* Jean."

Charles knew good and well that people are often raped by friends or dates or acquaintances, so Stewart's protest didn't mean much. But Stewart was upset, so Charles let him keep on talking instead of pointing this out.

"They went to fucking school together," continued Stewart, "in Conway. At Central Arkansas University. They were in the Honors Program together. And my brother would fuck with her sometimes. Just teasing, is all. Because he was a gun nut and a Republican, so she didn't approve of him. He had a Confederate flag hanging in his room, he liked to argue about how the South was no more racist than the North and the Civil War was purely a states'-rights issue, and he liked calling it the War for Southern Independence. Half the reason why he said shit like that was to get a rise out of people. And, you know, usually the liberals he'd argue with couldn't really beat him in a fair fight—their whole position basically was that he had to be wrong, because only terrible people thought that way.

"I mean, he fucked with me the same way—I'm a liberal too—I hate Bush—I'm going to vote for Obama. We got into some real fights over that stuff.

"That Jean girl thought that because he had a few automatic rifles he was responsible for every school shooting in America, and because he made a few off-color jokes he was responsible for all racial prejudice, and because he was a macho, traditionally masculine guy he must be a rapist. When half the time he was kidding, and the other half he was just making some good points that people don't like to hear. Myself included, I don't excuse myself. He was an independent thinker, he wasn't some thug. He was in the fucking Honors College!

"Anyway, she thought all this stuff about him. And as kind of a fuck-you, he would sometimes act like she was right.

"They wound up in Rogers for this big party over spring break. At somebody's house, way out, sort of in the countryside but not quite. They had a bonfire. That kind of party. Lots of beers.

"The next morning everyone took off someplace, except for Jean and my brother. Jean stayed because she was passed out. When she woke up she was freaked out to see Kevin was there. She was all freaked out to be alone with him. He was like, 'If I'd wanted to rape you I could have just done it while you were passed out.' And that freaked her out even more, even though it should have reassured her, because it was true if you think about it. Her being all afraid of him like he was some monster, it pissed him off, and to get back at her he pretended like she was right. He acted like he was chasing her around the house and everything, just playing. But she took him seriously, and she grabbed the gun that was in the bedroom nightstand and she shot him in the chest."

Stewart was done talking. He glared at Charles, defying him to challenge his account, then once again stared straight ahead.

Charles frowned and pondered. There was something odd about the story—nevertheless, it wasn't what he'd been expecting and that alone gave it the flavor of truth. "But if they were the only people at this house, how did you hear your brother's side of the story?" he asked, then realized what a blunt, asshole question that was. The fact was, Charles wasn't sure he wanted Stewart's version to be true. The idea that Jean had killed his brother to save herself from rape might be more dramatic, though that wasn't how he phrased it to himself.... Also, if he wound up believing Stewart's story, that might make it harder to talk to Marissa about it.

"That's *her* side," Stewart said. "That's the way *she* says it happened. Except for...." He got tangled up for a moment, frustrated with his inability to figure out the right way to say it. "I mean, you have to read between the lines of what she said, a little bit. But not much."

"What were her exact words about what happened?"

"I don't remember."

Neither one of them said anything.

Till Charles said, "So you think it was all a misunderstanding?"

"I think she had it in for him."

Charles's interest was reinvigorated. If Jean had been plotting to kill Stewart's brother all along! Charles's brain apprehended the idea through a veil of disbelief that would make it truly dazzling, if it proved to be true. "You think that she, like, was planning to do it?" he asked, a little breathlessly.

But now Stewart got flustered and confused again, and he said, "Maybe not exactly. Not consciously. But they were ... it was a thing with them. They weren't just two people who disagreed, there was a really intense thing between them. People had always said so, even before the thing happened. That's what they told us afterwards, anyway. I had never heard of her before he died, my brother never told me about her, because we didn't...."

Stewart trailed off without explaining why his brother had never told him about Jean.

The silence continued. Charles kept glancing over at Temple—if Stewart wouldn't worry about getting caught by Dan, Charles would worry on his behalf. Also it might be awkward for Charles if Dan got pissed at Stewart and at the same time saw Charles talking to him, even though Charles wasn't doing anything wrong.

As he was absorbing Stewart's tale, it occurred to Charles that they'd skipped over the most recent part of it. Tentatively, he said, "So, what about now, man? I mean, you moved to New York and now you work in the same building as her. That's kind of a weird coincidence. And Marissa said you asked her out on a date, without telling her who you were."

"Who's Marissa?"

Charles explained that Marissa was the redhead who'd yelled at Stewart the other day.

It was almost like Stewart had asked who Marissa was merely as a way of putting off having to answer the question. Charles figured the polite thing would be to drop the subject, if Stewart plainly didn't want to talk about it. But then he realized how badly he wanted to know. "So, like, how *did* you wind up in New York? How did you wind up on an OKCupid date with Jean?"

Stewart started to squirm, then caught himself and held still. "Just did," he said. After that he kind of clammed up. Soon Charles made up something he had to do, and left the park. Stewart stuck around a bit before leaving.

Stewart was still embarrassed as he rode the train home. When he'd started all this, it hadn't seemed worth the time to figure out how he would explain himself to people who found out about his situation. It hadn't even occurred to him that anyone would find anything out. He'd been alone in his room in Conway, looking at the scanty profiles of local girls, when he'd changed the settings to show him women from New York and idly scrolled through them: an embarrassing habit. And there had been Jean's photo, complete with her first name (though not her last, of course). He'd recognized her, naturally. Right away he'd announced he was moving to New York, giving no other reason than that he'd always sort of wanted to. He got a bus ticket for the next week and went on Craigslist and started looking for roommates. Bought a book on New York from the Travel section of Conway's bookstore and tried to study the maps. That book, a duffel bag with seven changes of clothes, a cheap laptop, his wallet, and his cell phone were all he brought with him to New York. The bus ride took three days and two nights. He got to see the country some. The morning he arrived, he called the number for the people in Queens he was renting a couch from. They said they would be there to let him in, as planned. With some work, he found the train he was supposed to be taking. Once the train came above-ground in Queens he was able to stare in awe at the skyline of New York, where he'd always dreamed of living.

His only plan had been to confront Jean. Not even to confront her, really: to haunt her. To not let her simply forget she'd murdered his brother, and go about her successful life. Landing the job and seeing her stroll in unsuspectingly to do her shopping had filled him with a violent, wrathful sweetness.

But he hadn't thought he would have to explain anything to anybody. *She* would know why he was here: that he was the ghost of his brother. And he would be able to be that by simply appearing before her, passively. *She* wouldn't want anyone to know who he was. All murderers want to keep their deeds secret, and he could count on her to isolate herself, in her shame and her terror.

Somehow it had never occurred to him that she would have the gall to act like she had nothing to hide; that she would herself believe the version she'd told the police. He'd assumed he would easily be able to go about making a life the unspoken purpose of which would be to become a weight on hers. Now it looked like he wasn't going to be able to keep the purpose so unspoken, after all. She was going to make him explain himself, on top of everything else she'd done. The fact outraged him, and left him feeling even more adrift now than before he'd left Arkansas.

Six

The next day was Stewart's day off. Charles worked the nine-to-five shift, and by chance left the store just as Marissa was leaving the building. He called after her—she paused to say hello and ask how he was. He didn't think it was his imagination that she was giving him an appraising look, as if she were still deciding what to do with him. Which would be good, he figured, since it meant she hadn't yet decided to blow him off.

She did keep glancing at the building entrance, and after a moment seemed to be trying to edge away. Charles hoped that was because Jean was still up there, and it would be awkward if she came out and saw Marissa talking to this guy who was friends with Stewart (and that it wasn't simply because he repulsed her). He said, "You know, I talked to Stewart."

"You did?" she said, her face getting livelier.

"Yeah. You want to, I don't know, um.... There's an Irish place a couple blocks away, called Muldoon's. If you wanted to get a beer and talk about it. Or maybe, like, dinner."

She thought it over. Charles waited. He had the impulse to say something like, "Or if you don't feel like it, that's fine too," but bit it back. He was trying to get out of the habit of saying stuff like that to women. If they wanted to reject him, fine, but let them do the work.

Marissa eyed him just long enough for it to be awkward. In the end she decided he wasn't bad. Besides, even if it did make her an evil nosey bitch, she really wanted to know more about this crazy thing that was going on. And she was afraid that if she bugged Jean about it, that would push her away and alienate her—so maybe she could just pump this guy till Jean felt like opening up.

They went to Muldoon's. Opening the door to the pub they were hit with a blast of off-key, fuzzily amplified caterwauling. Charles had never been here on a Thursday—apparently that was when they had karaoke on the schedule. The singer stood beside the door, oblivious to Charles and Marissa, drunkenly beaming at the lyrics on the TV screen as his friends from the office cheered. The song was "Wake Me Up Before You Go-Go," by Wham.

"Is this okay?" asked Charles, taking advantage of the noise to put his mouth close to her ear.

"Totally!" said Marissa, and turned to grin at him. "I fucking love shameless people."

They couldn't sit at the bar if they were going to hear each other over that karaoke; they asked for a table in the back, somewhat shielded from the noise, which necessitated ordering dinner. Charles couldn't really afford it, but it was worth it to be getting dinner with Marissa.

He told Marissa Stewart's side of the story. At first she was indignant. "So he claims his brother didn't even *do* anything?"

"Not exactly. He said Kevin was only *pretending* he was going to do something."

"Well, how was Jean supposed to know that?"

"That's kind of what I thought."

The waitress came over. She was genuinely Irish, like from Ireland. They ordered their beers, and each ordered nachos. Neither had realized the other was also going to order nachos, so they got some quick easy laughs out of that. The opening of Foreigner's "I Want to Know What Love Is" came blaring from the karaoke machine, along with the first few lyrics, passionately crooned by a drunk with what sounded like a cold, so they had some groans and laughs about that as well. By the time their beers arrived they were ready to settle back in to talking about Jean and Stewart, and Kevin. "Even if Kevin was 'only pretending' he was going to rape Jean, he deserved what he got," she pronounced. "Anyway, why would he do that? Only a person who was dangerous anyway would do that."

Charles was nodding. Even as he did so, however, he said, uncertainly, "Oh—I don't know...." Marissa bared her teeth at him a little. But he sensed that his best shot was to stick to his guns and not give in to her at the first pressure—besides, he did think she was possibly being not completely fair. "I don't mean Jean was wrong to shoot him if she thought he was a threat. I just mean it's not, you know, totally incomprehensible why he might have acted like that. Even though it's still wrong!"

"Enlighten me. Why might he have?"

"Well, you know. Stewart said he was, like, a macho guy. And kind of an asshole."

"Stewart said he was an asshole?"

"Not in so many words, but yeah, basically. An asshole, but not a bad guy. Like, a sexist, but not a *misogynist* exactly. And not a rapist, according to Stewart. Not a racist, but a guy who liked to tell racist jokes, to rile people up."

"Okay."

"But a guy like that.... The way Stewart told it, Jean really bought the show Kevin put on for people. Like, she took it more seriously than he meant people to. She thought he really was all those things. And maybe Kevin got offended, or even got his feelings hurt, even though of course it's his own fault if people think he really is what he pretends to be. Because guys who have this big asshole front, lots of times they're actually really sensitive, and the front is because they're insecure. So even though it's irrational, a guy like that might take offense that someone took him seriously. Because he's insecure and over-sensitive, which is the whole reason for the front in the first place. And if he isn't willing to admit to himself that that's the dynamic, he's that much more likely to get mad at Jean and want to get back at her, for having thought he was such a bad guy. And the way he does that is to act like she's right. To him, the point probably was that she'd feel stupid once she realized how totally harmless he actually was. He didn't realize she couldn't tell the difference between his acting-out, and the real thing."

Marissa said, "Okay," not as if she were necessarily accepting his theory, but as if she would consider it. She looked like she was fine-tuning her evaluation of Charles, too. "You must be pretty sensitive, yourself, to rattle off a psych profile like that."

"Well. I don't know how sensitive I am. I mean, I still think it sounds like he engineered a situation where Jean was totally within her rights to shoot him."

"No, I don't mean 'sensitive' as in 'you old dumb softie,' I mean it as in 'smart,' 'perceptive,' stuff like that."

"Oh. Okay. In that case."

There was a group singing "Bohemian Rhapsody," and they'd gotten to the baroque part right before the hard-rock freakout, the part with all the "Scaramouche" stuff, and they were falling all over each other and generally fucking up. Charles and Marissa laughed, and mocked the singers for a bit, until Marissa hoisted her beer and said, "How many drinks'll it take to get you up there singing with me?"

"More than I can afford." Immediately Charles wished he hadn't said that. Hopefully, Marissa would think he was only joking (even though it was true). She did kind of laugh a little as she swigged her beer, which was nearly half-gone.... He would definitely have to pay both their tabs now, just to prove he could. Fuck the rent.

They went back to talking about Kevin, Stewart, and Jean, although Charles was looking for ways to broaden the scope of the conversation and refocus it on himself and Marissa, so as not to get irretrievably trapped in this gossipy ghetto. Hoping it might prove to be a useful, smooth transition, he said, "I feel like I knew guys like that back home."

"Where are you from?" asked Marissa, as he'd hoped she would.

"Spokane."

She evinced interest. They talked about Spokane a while, about how it wasn't near Seattle, about how he might love it but he didn't like it. He asked where she was from.

"D.C.," she said.

"The halls of power," he intoned. She made a face like that wasn't necessarily funny, but like she was finding him cute anyway.

They got refills on their beers, and continued to evolve the conversation. Before their nachos were done they'd ordered a third round of drinks. Charles didn't know how he was going to eat for the next week after he paid for all of this, and was telling himself that he better get a lay out of it, if not tonight then eventually.

She asked what it was like getting his MFA from Sarah Lawrence.

"Meh," said Charles. "I mainly did it as an excuse to move to New York like I'd always wanted. In retrospect I wish I'd just moved here and written. Would've been cheaper."

"But now you'll always have that diploma," Marissa pointed out.

Charles was on the verge of saying, *Yeah, right, and I'm putting it to good use working for minimum wage*, but reminded himself not to harp on his low economic status when flirting. Why undo with one dumb remark whatever he might accomplish by paying for dinner?

She asked if he still did any writing. "Yeah," he said, "I go up to the Hungarian Pastry Shop and work on stuff."

"The Hungarian Pastry Shop? What's that?"

"You don't know the Hungarian Pastry Shop?!"

Marissa drew herself up in mock offense. "Do I look like a woman who spends much time in pastry shops?"

"It's a coffee shop, mainly. Up by Columbia. It's famous for, uh … well, there's a lot of graffiti in the bathroom, from Columbia students mostly, like this super-witty pretentious graffiti."

"You're really selling this place."

"No, come on, you should go. It's just good coffee, and no radio playing, and people writing and reading and talking. I take it back about the pretentiousness, it's actually really authentic.

Like, you know those sorts of places that were part of your original daydreamy reasons for moving to New York? It's one of the last places like that, that hasn't closed yet."

They ordered more beers to wash down the last of their nachos. From the front of the bar came crashing the noise of yet another drunken chorus, this time howling their way through "Born to Run." Marissa leaned forward and fixed upon Charles her manically gleaming eyes, and laughed. Charles laughed, too.

"Can I make a confession?" she said.

"Uh-oh."

"I love karaoke."

"So go up there. You couldn't possibly be worse than these guys."

"You wanna do it together?"

Shit. "It might take another beer or two."

"Oh, come on, don't be a wimp."

"Oh ho, is this a challenge?"

"Yeah, it's a challenge. It's a dare."

"Okay, so I accept this dare, but you'll have to accept another dare in the future, of equal or greater value."

"What dare is that?"

"To be determined."

"So basically just a blank check."

"In exchange for singing karaoke in this crowded Irish bar? Yup, that's what I want."

They drained the last of their mugs and Marissa insisted they go sign up right away—no reprieves. Oh well, if they were singing instead of drinking, he'd save some money at least. There was a harmlessly malicious edge to the grin and wink Marissa gave him. Who knew if anything would come of it, even a make-out session; for the moment it was pleasurable enough just to be her plaything.

Seven

Jean continued popping into Temple Books as she'd always done. She made a point of going just as often as ever, albeit without the same relaxation as before; not at first, anyway. She didn't go on any more big sprees—it was wasteful, plus she found piles of books you don't have time to read depressing. So after that one time she no longer tried to flaunt her greater economic power. To begin with she would pointedly ignore Stewart. But soon she could flip through books again for minutes at a time with hardly a thought of him. He also soon seemed able to go about his work without being excessively preoccupied with her.

She got used to seeing him there. Once she started thinking the whole thing over in the absence of adrenaline, it became a little less egregious, although still kind of nuts. He never threatened her or anything—to be honest, he never had. She could understand why Stewart would be fucked up over his big brother being killed, even though she refused to feel guilty. It wasn't like Stewart had known his brother was a rapist, or anything. It even would be understandable for him to refuse to believe Kevin had ever tried to rape her.

After all, Kevin hadn't always been such a bad guy, though it had been hard to remember that ever since the thing had happened. Or rather, it had never occurred to her to remember it till she started seeing Stewart around. He brought those early days back, so that sometimes she was even able to recall them almost without the taint of the intervening trauma. They'd had some laughs, her and Kevin. Early on.

One day, about three weeks after her date with Stewart, she was at Temple, leaning her shoulder against one of the shelves, flipping through a volume of Proust and wondering if it would be worth it to forego the time needed to read ten other books instead, just to banish her sense of failure at not having read Proust. Stewart appeared before her with some books to shelve. He glanced up but seemed hardly to register her. That was how accustomed they'd gotten to seeing each other. It was crazy—she wondered which of them was Jane Goodall and which the chimp.

For no particular reason, she let her eyes stay on Stewart after he'd looked away; she was mulling over this weird connection they had, and reflecting that the most bizarre part was how it had become part of their everyday lives.

Stewart noticed she was looking at him and looked up at her in turn.

Without thinking it over first, Jean smiled faintly and in a soft voice said, "Hi."

From his face you would have thought she'd told him to go fuck his mother. For a few seconds Jean could pretend she was misreading him, since he seemed unable to find his voice to say anything. Maybe she should have looked away, but it was hard not to keep an eye on someone who was staring at you like that.

Finally he walked up to her. When he came to a halt he was already too close. She stood her ground. "What did you say to me?" he demanded, in a tightly-controlled growl.

"I said 'Hey,'" she said, tightening down her gut and clamping her feet to the floor in preparation for a fight, keeping the book between him and her.

"And why did you say that?" he asked. "Why did you say 'Hey' to me?"

"Because I saw you standing there and decided to try being civil."

Jean had reasoned out, over the last couple weeks, that even if Stewart did lose his shit and attack her, he probably wouldn't seriously hurt her and she would be able to use the event to press charges or at least get a restraining order against him. Not that a restraining order was likely to do much good. Anyway, that certainly wasn't very comforting now, when it looked like he really was going to slap her. She resolved not to flinch unless he actually went for her, and hoped she still looked steady and unafraid.

She was succeeding better than she could have guessed. So much so that her cool, distant, aloof face was taken by Stewart for contempt, and nearly really did goad him into hitting her.

He said, "Why would you be civil to me? Are we friends or something?"

He was speaking in a low hiss, keeping their conversation private. They were between two shelves, hidden from the cashiers and the front of the store. Instead of answering loudly enough to draw attention, and to draw help in case Stewart did flip out, Jean automatically matched his volume: "No, but I figured I may as well try it since apparently we're going to be seeing each other all the time, thanks to you."

"It's not supposed to be pleasant for you!"

"Are your feelings hurt because I'm not mad enough that you're stalking me?"

He blinked like his eyes were stinging, and she wondered if he was going to cry. Fine, fuck him.

She said, "I'm a human being, not some animal you're tracking."

"How can you not even feel bad about it?" From the way his voice crackled, she thought he might soon have to start shouting in order to keep from crying. But for now both of them continued to speak in rough whispers.

"How I feel about what happened to me is none of your business. The same way how you feel about him is none of mine. If you want to talk about how you feel then I guess maybe I'll listen. But I do not want to talk about how I feel."

"My dead brother is none of my business?"

"What happened between me and him in Rogers is not any of...." Jean faltered and trailed off, because the shooting death of his brother manifestly was Stewart's business. And yet the memory of what had happened felt deeply personal ... or maybe "personal" was the wrong word, given how endlessly she'd repeated her account, under official circumstances. But through it all she had held on fiercely to her sense that she owned the events, that they were hers to interpret. Not to fabricate, she had been scrupulously honest, but she would not let anyone twist the interpersonal and ethical dynamics to suit some other agenda, to make out like what Kevin had been doing hadn't been so bad and she'd overreacted. Kevin had been asking for it. She was offended and confused that the mere presence of his brother should be enough to weaken that certainty, emotionally if not intellectually.

So instead of finishing her sentence, she said, "What is it you want from me?"

"I want you to regret it."

"Is that a threat?"

"No. Jesus. I want you to regret having killed that human being, the way any normal person would."

Now she was the one having to blink against the stinging of her eyes. "And what about what he was gonna do to me, huh? Who gets to regret that?"

"No one, now. He would have, if you'd given him a chance." In a tone as if he were reminding himself that he had to be patient with her, because of how stupid she was, he said, "He was only kidding around. I'm not saying what he did was right, but he never would have really hurt you."

"I'm sure you're right. He just would have held me down and fucked me when I didn't want him to."

"He would never have done that! He was only kidding!"

"Hey, you weren't there, you didn't see his face."

"Yeah, well now I never will," he snapped.

After that they stood glaring at each other and breathing hard. *This is ridiculous,* Jean thought.

"Listen," she said, in a carefully calm voice. A customer wandered into earshot, and Jean and Stewart watched him uncomfortably, waiting for him to go. He picked up on the vibe and looked at them in surprise, then moved away to leave them their space.

"Listen," she said again. Then, again, she stopped. She'd been about to say, "We have to find a way to live with each other." But why? He was just a guy who worked in the bookstore downstairs, he wasn't likely to work there forever. And it wasn't like she would be in her current job the rest of her life, either. Who cared whether she and Stewart got along? Couldn't she simply ignore him?

But when he spoke again, still with that intense glare fixed on her, it was like she'd spoken her thought aloud and he was responding to it. "I didn't come up here to live in harmony with you," he said. "I'm not exactly sure of the details of why I came, but it definitely wasn't that."

"As far as I can tell you came here so you could make me feel bad."

"Yeah. Thanks, that's it—I just couldn't figure out the right way to phrase it. But yeah, I moved up here to make you feel bad."

"Is that really the only reason you came?"

"The only one you need to worry about."

For a while they continued merely to look at each other. But there was no reason to keep doing that, so Jean left.

Back in her cubicle, she didn't think the encounter had bothered her much. In fact, a few times she said to herself, *Poor Stewart.* But when she left work and walked to Grand Central, she kept peering compulsively over her shoulder. She kept it up even once she was walking home from her station. Even once she was back in her apartment with the door locked.

Her right hand was shaking. To still it she gripped it with her left. Her ears were ringing, as if the gunshots had only now exploded in front of her, instead of six years ago. How loud they'd been! And the way Kevin had gone sailing backwards so slowly, his arms overhead and outstretched, so that she'd wondered what he was doing till she'd realized he was falling because she'd shot him. In her head she knew he must not have fallen slowly at all, but that was the way she remembered it. And there had been all that blood.

She tried to read but it was impossible to concentrate so she put the book down. Only then did she realize it was one of the books she'd bought when she was showing off to Stewart.

She flipped open her laptop and called up Netflix. There was a long queue of foreign movies she'd been meaning to watch, but she didn't feel like seeing anything real and decided to just watch "Frasier."

The laugh tracks droned. When she'd shot Kevin, blood had splattered back onto her.

Even if she did get a new job, or Stewart left his, he would keep putting himself in her line of sight as long as she let him. So she couldn't let him.

Eight

Jean had been talking to people back home about the whole Stewart thing—a very select few people, anyway. Like her old best friend Penny.

Jean and Penny had been friends in high school, but Penny had gone to college in Louisiana. During those four years they'd drifted apart slightly, then reconnected after graduation. Jean wasn't in touch much with the friends she'd had in the Honors College, in Conway. Most everyone had believed her account of what had happened, but Kevin had had an undeniable charisma and, despite his abrasive antics, lots of people had liked him. There had been a certain ambiguity to the whole shooting/rape situation. Anyway, even though her friends had on the whole been perfectly willing to be supportive of her, after they were done being supportive they generally had not seemed keen on hanging out any further. Kevin's friends, of course, had generally *not* been supportive. Penny had never met Kevin.

Jean called Penny the Saturday after her encounter at Temple with Stewart and tried to describe the meeting, but couldn't quite put it into words satisfactorily. Penny was saying for the thousandth time that Jean should call the police and inform them of what was going on, "just in case." This was undoubtedly true, but Jean felt embarrassed at the thought of calling the cops on Stewart when he technically hadn't done much, yet.

Apropos of nothing, Jean said, "I'm thinking of moving out of the city."

"What?!" exclaimed Penny; then, with a gleam of hope, "Back to Arkansas?"

"*No*. Like, to Westchester, maybe. That's north of the city. Or even to Pennsylvania, and commuting."

"Oh.... Jean, honey, you're not letting Kevin's brother run you off, are you?"

"Oh, no. No. I just finally miss having a yard, is all."

After she got off the phone she went online and started looking for a place, preferably a stand-alone home, one where somebody could walk right up to the front door. As she clicked through the sites of various realtors, looking at the pictures, it came to her that, actually, she really did miss having a yard. Maybe she should even think about getting a mortgage and buying a place, though the idea was kind of freaky. She made some calls and got some appointments to look at places in Stroudsburg, Pennsylvania. Why delay?

For a second she felt excited about the proposed life-change, the trees and space and all that. Then she remembered what her actual plan was, and it was like all the guts in her lower belly suddenly hardened to solid ice.

She got a shower and went to Jersey City. Walking to the train she used her smartphone to call up a list of Jersey City gun shops.

Once at the gun shop, she felt a strange tumult. Though fluorescents, the lights seemed somehow warm. It felt like being back in Arkansas. But that was strange, because even in Arkansas she'd never been in a gun shop. Her family had been one of the few she'd known of growing up that hadn't kept guns in the house, and she herself had always been more or less against them, and had considered New York's anti-gun laws one of the perks of living there.

Even now, looking uncertainly around the gun shop, she was against them. Even that one day in Rogers, she'd been against them as a general principle. If Kevin had paused long enough to challenge her by saying something like, "Oh, I see all of a sudden you're pro-gun," she would have denied it. She remembered that when she shot him, she'd been studying Kant's categorical imperative for a class. According to the categorical imperative, you were supposed to act as if each one of your actions obeyed an ideal universal law. If Jean had believed that the world was a place where practicing the categorical imperative made sense, would do some good, then she supposed she wouldn't have shot Kevin, or else she would have felt bad about it later. But, regardless of whether or not she personally was or was not predisposed towards seeing the universe through the lens of ethical considerations, there was no denying the fact that this was a world of special cases, and that when push came to shove there was something a little ridiculous about insisting on abstract principles when the stakes were so concrete.

Really, it was strange how familiar the store felt. If you raised a seagull from the day it hatched in some aviary in a deeply inland zoo, and then one day opened under its beak a sealed bottle filled with sea air, giving the bird a whiff, who knew what would stir inside it. The place had a smell, with a chemical crispness to it. Like a grandmother's mothballed closet you would sneak your head into sometimes as a kid.

The guy behind the counter had mutton chops and a soul patch, and a long gray ponytail. His T-shirt was stretched tight over his big belly and tucked into his jeans. "Can I help you?" he asked, looking his cute customer up and down without quite being a dickhead about it.

Jean went up to the counter and said she was interested in something for home defense. The guy showed her a revolver. The main thing she noticed about it was that it didn't look like the gun she'd shot Kevin with.

He was explaining stuff to her about the gun. She said, "Can it shoot through a door?"

He gave her a funny look, like how cute she was was no longer the primary thing he was thinking about. "Why would you want to shoot through a door?"

"Like, if someone were trying to break it down."

"Depends how thick the door is."

She told the guy that right now she was living in Queens,

but that she was moving to Pennsylvania really soon, and asked if he could go ahead and start a background check using her current address.

No, the guy told her. It was illegal for him to sell a gun to someone out of state. But he told her about an upcoming Pennsylvania gun show where she would have no problem buying one. There would be private citizens there selling their goods—unlike licensed dealers such as himself, private citizens didn't have to run background checks or anything.

By Monday, when she returned to work, the ball was already rolling for her to move to Stroudsburg in a month—she had appointments to look at a couple of places. It was exhilarating to be making such big changes so fast, and so impulsively. She'd decided to rent for the moment, instead of trying to buy. Partly because she objectively knew that applying for a mortgage on a lark would be crazy, partly because if she rented she could move sooner.

Marissa came by after lunch and stood over Jean, at her computer. "Want to go out for some margaritas after work? Or is Monday too early in the week to start drinking?"

"Monday is the perfect day for it," Jean said.

They talked like they might go someplace nice and respectable but wound up walking west to Chevy's at Times Square, laughing all the way at how trashy they were. The Mexican food was relatively cheap, for Times Square. The margaritas were big. The restaurant's bright colors, noise, and plastic gaiety were fun to laugh at. "It's better than some stuffy bullshit!" declared Marissa, gulping down her cherry margarita.

Jean had gotten a normal-flavored margarita, though they were both jumbo. "Hey, you don't have to justify your love of Chevy's to me." Of the two of them, Marissa had been the more enthusiastic about going there.

Half an hour later they were both stuffed, with their plates still more than half-full, and they were each well into their second jumbo margaritas. Marissa had decided to mix it up and try a raspberry-flavored one.

"I love these things!" said Marissa, lifting the massive heavy glass up to her face. It wasn't much smaller than her head. "Because they're like my name. Get it?! Margarita, Marissa!"

"Oh, God. We're going to get totally shit-faced, aren't we?"

"No, no, no, I'm fine, I'm fine." Marissa took a moment to regain control of herself, but also to drink some more. There was a lull, despite the blaring music, and on the other side of the lull they found the mood had changed. Marissa tucked her chin and looked up at Jean seriously; "How are you doing?" she asked. "With that thing?"

"With Stewart?"

"Is that his name? The guy from the bookstore? The Arkansan?"

"Yeah. Stewart."

"Well?"

Jean drained the last of her margarita; the straw made a dry croaking sound, and she signaled the waitress for another. She was light-headed, if not frankly drunk. But she'd already gone too far to do anything productive tonight, so she might as well say fuck it and go all the way. When she turned to look across the table again, Marissa was still waiting for an answer, with her serious expression on. "I think I'm moving out of the city," Jean said, trying to be breezy about it.

Marissa's face fell. "Because of *Stewart?*" she said. "Jean, you don't have to be scared of him! We can do something about him!"

"No, no, no." Jean was flustered—she'd intended her comment as a change of subject. "No, it's not that. I'm just moving to Stroudsburg. In Pennsylvania."

"Well why would anyone move to Buttfuck, Pennsylvania unless they were being chased there?"

Thirty seconds ago Jean had thought she was stuffed, but now she found herself picking through her refried beans, lifting a forkful to her mouth, and swallowing it, only to have a reason to put off answering. She said, "Grass. Also, the gun laws are different there. So...."

Marissa stared at her as if she were not only crazy, but perhaps morally repugnant as well. "You're going to get a *gun*?"

"Well. Why not?"

"If you think you need a gun then it sounds like you're not doing so well with the whole bookstore-guy thing. It sounds like you're scared of him."

"Once I have a gun I'll be significantly less scared. Besides, I'm not scared. I'm just trying to be cautious. Responsible."

"If you think you're unsafe then you need to call the police."

"Yeah, well, except he's not doing anything illegal. All right, Marissa? And neither will I be if I move to Stroudsburg and get a gun. Now can we talk about something else please?"

They gossiped about work through most of their third margaritas, but their hearts weren't in it. Gazing on the last inch or two of her drink, slurring her words, Marissa said, "Wanna share a cab home?"

"You live in Brooklyn. I live in Queens."

"Fuck." Marissa gazed sullenly out the window at the taxi- and tourist-clogged street. It wasn't even dark yet.

Jean had again started picking through her food and absently eating it. Also slurring her words a little, she said, "You know, the thing about having a gun...."

She stopped. Marissa waited for her to start again, eyes fixed on her, all ears.

Jean was evacuating her rice to the part of her plate already occupied by her half-eaten, cooled burrito. Keeping her eyes on the food, as if this were an operation of great importance, she said, "Having a gun, when you live alone someplace ... I mean, you know, you're allowed to defend yourself."

"Sure."

"And this way, it's kind of like Stewart gets to choose."

Marissa waited for her to keep talking and, when she realized she wasn't going to, said, "Choose what?"

"Well, you know. The scary thing about Stewart is ... I mean, it's not even scariness. It's just anxiety. Wondering, like, what's he going to do? If he just wants to work at the bookstore and live in the city, that's his business, I can live with that. But if he's going to hurt me, I'd rather just find out that's what he's got in mind and get it over with. So I'll get a place in Stroudsburg. I'll get a gun, just so I'm safe. I'll make sure Stewart knows where my new place is. And if he comes up there, trying to trespass, trying to force his way in … then I'll know."

Marissa stared at Jean, scrunching up her eyebrows, not certain she'd followed all that. "Then you'll know … what?"

"What he's got in mind."

Still Marissa stared at her, trying to digest it. "What do you mean, you'll make sure Stewart knows where your new place is? Wouldn't you rather he didn't know?"

"He'll know where it is. And then, if he comes, I'll know what his intentions are. And I'll be able to handle it."

There was a fairly long silence between them. Sounding a little more sober, Marissa said, "That sounds almost like you're setting him up."

Jean's eyes leapt up to meet hers, sharp, angry, and shocked. "I don't see how that makes sense." Immediately, an embarrassed cloud muddled her face, as if she'd replayed her own words to herself and wondered if she'd inadvertently exposed something, or discovered something.

Marissa felt more confused and uncomfortable than she had in a long while. It didn't help that objects were starting to slip out of their proper places in her field of vision. Seconds ago she'd been toying with the idea of ordering yet another margarita, but now she was glad her glass was empty and she would be able to leave soon. Still, she felt like she had to say, "That's just kind of what it sounded like."

"I'm just moving to someplace where I'm allowed to defend myself. You're the one who's been talking about how worried I should be." She paused, waiting for Marissa to agree with her. When she wouldn't, Jean signaled the waitress for the bill. "I need to get home," she said.

They managed to maintain their balance on the way out. The light was the sharp blue of early evening, punctuated by

LED screens splashing advertisements and by the colors of the cars and people. Marissa said, "Do you want to split a cab?"

"We talked about this. I live in Queens, you live in Brooklyn."

"Oh. Yeah." Marissa's nauseating sense of being unmoored and adrift, which she'd thought was ebbing, surged back stronger than ever. She resolved to keep her mouth shut until her head cleared and she had a chance to think about what was going on.

Nine

Stewart, too, would call his friend from home. Her name was Maggie and they'd dated in high school and part of his first year of college; after breaking up they'd remained best friends. She'd only met Kevin a few times, because by the time she and Stewart started hanging out Kevin was already in college.

Maggie was sympathetic towards Stewart, but exasperated with him, and worried. She was afraid he was liable to get himself arrested somehow.

"I keep telling you," she said to him over the phone, not unkindly but firmly, "there's a reason they didn't press charges against her."

"I understand that. I understand all the legal stuff. But I know he was never planning to do anything bad to her."

"Sure," said Maggie, with fraying indulgence. Stewart had explained to her many, many times his theory about how Kevin had only been acting out. In the past few months it had seemed to obsess him more and more—instead of fading with the years, his grief and rage had suddenly surged back. "I believe you're probably right about what was going through Kevin's mind. But even if you are right, you can't prove in court what was in his head."

"I know that. But she was there. She knew better."

"You can't prove what was in her head, either." The first hundred times she'd said this over the years, she'd been less blunt about it.

Instead of replying Stewart chewed his lips. He was certain that his brother had been goofing around and Jean had overreacted.

The silence stretched on. Finally Maggie said, with a tired helplessness, "So how's the rest of your life? Are you enjoying New York at all?"

Begrudgingly, he told her about some of the cool stuff he'd been doing. For example, he'd discovered you could go to the opera for fifteen bucks, if you sat in the back row. The fucking opera! His horizons were being expanded, but they would have expanded more if he didn't always have the Jean thing tugging at his mind.

He couldn't help but talk about it again. "I just want people to know that Kevin wasn't going to do anything bad. If she'd just talked to him and told him to quit, instead of fucking shooting him."

"I think she did tell him to quit, Stewart."

"Yeah, but I'm sure she said it like, 'Stop it, you dumb monster,' which would only egg him on. If she'd talked to him like a fellow human, things would have been different."

There was another long silence. He started to worry. Sure enough, when Maggie did speak again, she said, "I love you, Stewart, but do you ever hear yourself anymore?"

It was true, Stewart privately conceded, he might be a little crazy. He said, "She was just a little trigger-happy. It's not entirely her fault. I understand that she was scared. But she was just a little trigger-happy. I just want people to realize that. Or, if even just she realized it, that would be enough."

"All right, Stewart," said Maggie, a little loudly, her patience momentarily depleted. "I hate to say this, but if you pretend you're going to rape someone, you kind of can't complain if she believes you and reacts accordingly." Stewart hung up on her.

The next day at work was one of his sullen, distant days. His coworkers had grown accustomed to these. Charles didn't try to reach out to him, the way he still would have a week ago. For one thing, he was bonding steadily with the other workers, and so had less need of Stewart—though he remained interested in the guy's saga, and was always toying with ideas on how to draw him out about it.

Charles was standing under the Information sign and Peter was at the register beside him, when Stewart walked up holding his hand on his belly. "Hey, Peter," he said, ignoring Charles, making a pitiful face, "I'm not feeling so good, I think maybe I ought to go home."

Without looking at Stewart, Peter smiled faintly and shook his head. In a gentle voice he said, "I don't know, man. You haven't been working here long and you've already gone home sick twice."

Stewart blushed. "But I'm sick," he said.

"You can do what you need to do, man. All I'm saying is, I don't know what Daniel will do if he hears you've gone home for the third time while you're still in your first month."

Stewart stared at him, red-faced and at a loss, hand forgotten on his belly. Charles was embarrassed too, for Stewart's sake, and kept his eyes forward. After a few seconds Stewart slunk off, and didn't mention being sick again. On this day he and Charles were on the same shift, but when their workday was over Charles shot the shit a while with his co-workers, whereas Stewart took off.

Finally, Charles left the store. As if his brain was keyed to track her, he immediately noticed Marissa crossing the street from Bryant Park. He was trying to decide the best way to attract her attention, when to his delight he realized she was already waving at him. He waved back and waited with a smile for her at the crosswalk.

But well before she arrived, he saw that she wasn't smiling. On the other hand, she said, "I was waiting over there for you to come out." That was good, presumably.

She really looked unhappy, though. Charles wondered if there had been some sort of weird, impossible-to-predict ramifications from their night of karaoke. Then he remembered how they'd met and realized that it probably had to do with Stewart.

"Can I talk to you?" she asked.

"Sure. You want to go someplace? Get a beer? Maybe Muldoon's again?"

"How about someplace quieter?"

"Sure."

As they walked he was scrambling to think of some nearby bar that might be quiet. Luckily Marissa said she knew a place and she led the way there. As they entered Charles glanced at the price list by the front door and was relieved to see that he could expect to survive the evening, albeit with injuries.

At least they sat at the bar, so there wouldn't be a waiter to tip. Once they'd each ordered their beer, Charles said, "So. What's up?"

"Um." Marissa was tearing up the cardboard coaster in front of her, making a face like she was in physical pain.

Charles began to worry about her, actually. "Hey," he said, lightly and cautiously placing his fingertips on her arm. "What is it?" The bartender started to put their beers down in front of them, stopped and scowled when he saw what Marissa had done to her coaster, and replaced it before setting down her drink.

Charles waited as Marissa fished around for the right words. "Have you talked to Stewart any more?" she asked at last. "About that thing?"

"No. Not really."

"What do you think about him?"

"You mean, like, do I think he's a good guy?"

"Yeah. Kind of. Pretty much."

"Well. I mean, of course there's all that stuff you told me about, with the stalking and everything...."

"Right, yeah, but aside from that."

"Aside from that, he seems all right. Kind of intense. I would like him fine, except some of that stuff you told me about makes me wary."

Marissa nodded, taking this in, nursing her beer.

Charles didn't see how he'd said anything complicated enough to need taking in. "Why do you ask?" he prompted.

"Well, I like Jean too, a lot. She's a friend. I mean, you know, a work friend."

"Okay." Then: "Yeah, she sounds nice."

"She is. She's cool. She's just...." Marissa hesitated, and when she spoke again it was in a tone like she wanted to remind Charles that it was *his* friend, not hers, who was ultimately responsible for whatever was going on: "I just really think this whole thing with Stewart is messing with her head!"

"Well. I can understand how it would."

Marissa outlined Jean's plan to go to Stroudsburg, get a gun, and wait for Stewart to come up there to her so she could, presumably, shoot him.

Charles stared at her. "Well ... I mean, I guess it sounds like she would only shoot him if he, like, came up there after her?... Which surely he wouldn't really do...."

"Yeah, but what if she said something to him? Something to lure him up there so she could shoot him?"

Well, that sounded like it would be murder.

Charles wasn't ready to use the word "murder," though. Instead, he said, "You mean sort of like killing him on purpose?"

"Maybe. I don't know. Probably not."

They sat there in silence.

Marissa said, "It's just, I think she's really freaked out by Stewart. I think she's scared of him. And people do crazy shit when they're scared."

"Right. Right."

Marissa was running her gently-closed fingers over the glass, stroking it up and down. Her face not only looked like she might possibly be in pain, Charles realized; she looked like she really might cry. He tried to think of some way to keep her from doing so.

It was too late. Her face crumpled as she said, "I don't want to feel like I'm *bad*-mouthing her or anything.... I mean, when you think of everything she's been *going* through," and she choked out some sobs.

Charles wasted a few seconds wondering what she was crying for, before taking advantage of the opportunity to press his palm gently against her back and rub it in slow circles. "Hey," he said, "hey now. No one thinks you're bad-mouthing her. Everybody understands." He quickly added, "Everybody who knows about this, I mean. Which as far as I know is just me. I haven't told anybody." It was plain enough why she was crying: partly, no doubt, because she felt stressed out by the whole situation; but also in order to amp up the emotion. If she wasn't officially an actress then that was only because the theater was too small a stage for her when the whole world was sitting there available; and like a true ham, she didn't care which character the script wanted to highlight, if she was in the scene then it was hers. Charles, whose favorite actor was William Shatner, had a thing for hams. He rubbed her back, feeling the smooth bones of her ribs and spine through the red, sheer fabric, the kind of fabric only females get to wear, a fact which for some men makes it nearly as erotic as those body parts that only females get to have. Charles widened the circles of his arm, letting his hand finally hook onto her neck, where his fingers consolingly caressed the nape, while his other hand came to rest on her forearm. Experimentally, he pulled her towards him, and she let her head rest obligingly against his chest. He stroked his fingers through her curly thick hair and whispered, "Shhh, shhh." She was one of those girls who liked drama. Well, sex and romance might not always be the very most effective spurs to drama, but Charles was confident they were well up there, and from the way Marissa was burrowing her head into his chest it looked like she thought so too. Charles knew that girls like that could be wild and unpredictable—a fight could be as dramatic as sex—a girl might decide actually fucking him was less dramatic than calling the whole thing off right before fucking him. But it was worth the ride, because Charles fucking relished that shit. It was the only time he felt truly alive, to use the cliché. He tucked his head down, lifted his hand from her forearm to touch her chin and tip it back, doing everything gently so as not to destroy the delicate equilibrium, and slowly lowered his head to hers and tasted her mouth before the universe could stop him.

They made out for a while, and Charles felt good about where they stopped—it wasn't like Marissa called it off because she was getting bored or irritated, it was more like they both mutually drifted away from it because if they progressed much further it would become something it was embarrassing to do in public. This bar was apparently a hang-out of Marissa's, after all (Charles loved it when girls demonstrated they didn't mind being seen with you by making out with you in public on their own turf). She remained leaning against him, letting him put his arm around her shoulders and caress her right arm with his thumb while they drank their second round.

They talked about her work. Charles preferred that to talking about his, because he was afraid of reminding her how much less money he made than she did—but she drew him out on the subject of his job and he told some stories that made her laugh. Charles could be a funny guy, particularly when inspired by the presence of a woman. That was probably his main strength.

Eventually, she said, "So what do you think I ought to do about the thing with Jean and Stewart and the gun?" She was much calmer about it now, probably because of all the energy she'd expended in crying and making out.

"I'm not sure what we can do about it," he said, using the first-person plural in the hopes of acclimating her to the idea of thinking of the two of them as a couple, as a pair who had dealings with each other.

She recoiled from him slightly. "We need to do something if we think she might kill him."

In the excitement Charles had forgotten that the stakes had gotten that high. Now he remembered, and pictured with distant horror a world in which he allowed Stewart to get shot. "What should we do, though? I guess I should warn Stewart?"

"Well, but I don't want it to get back to her that I've been talking about her behind her back."

Charles mulled it over. Warning Stewart that Jean might be setting a trap to kill him, without letting him know why Charles thought so, seemed like a tall order. Then again, if that was the task Marissa wanted to set for her champion or whatever, then so be it. "I'll figure something out," he said.

As a reward, she nestled against him. The noise and bustle of the bar continued around them. The commotion was not an intrusion of the world, but a cocoon protecting himself and Marissa from it.

Marissa's cheek stirred against him; not restlessly; she was nuzzling.

Charles risked lowering his mouth to her ear and murmuring, "I'm really sorry about everything that's going on between Stewart and Jean, but I'm also glad it gave us a reason to talk to each other in the first place."

It gave him a thrill to dance so recklessly along the blade of her irony and sophistication. Breath bated, he watched to see what she would do; he let the air out in relief when, instead of ignoring his sappiness or rolling her eyes at it, she rotated her face up towards his again and smiled at him, and held her mouth there for him as he bent down to kiss it.

Ten

A couple weeks went by and Charles didn't find an opportune time to warn Stewart about Marissa's suspicions. Away from her and the sexual field she generated, her fears seemed far-fetched. Just because Jean was moving to Stroudsburg was no reason to assume she was plotting murder. And as a guy from the West, Charles found nothing particularly ominous about the idea that she would want to get a gun, once she was living someplace where they were legal. It had been thirteen days since their thing at the bar, and in that time he and Marissa had had one date, on the weekend. The date had been warm, fun, and lively, and Charles believed Marissa when she said her job was too busy just now for her to meet him this week. Maybe she was dating other guys, too—Charles could understand that. However, if they were only going to see each other once a week then it was frustrating that they hadn't had sex yet. If they had to wait until the fourth date or whatever, then at this rate Marissa might easily lose interest in him beforehand.

On their date she'd asked if he'd broached with Stewart the subject of Jean's possible trap. Charles had admitted he hadn't, and had fended off her reproaches. He figured that if he acquiesced too easily and showed no resistance at all, Marissa was likely to get bored with him soon. That said, he reflected that, after all, it was a worrisome possibility, and he kept a sharper eye out for moments to bring the subject up with Stewart.

Meanwhile, Jean had already moved to a place she found in Stroudsburg. She and her roommate Helen had parted amicably, since Helen had been able to quickly find a replacement roommate. Jean and Helen had had a little goodbye party Jean's last night in the apartment—just the two of them, plus four beers—and had promised each other to meet soon for drinks. They'd both been wondering if they really would.

She'd gone to that gun show the guy at the Jersey City gun shop had recommended. It would be lying to say there hadn't been an element of fun to it. It had been an adventure, renting a car and finding her way along the highway to the nondescript town and its convention center. With trepidation she'd walked into that big bustling warehouse of a building, feeling as if she were trying to infiltrate a bevy of extra-terrestrials in a flimsy rubber-suit disguise. But if the denizens of this other world did notice that she didn't belong, it only inspired them to be especially nice to her. And that gave Jean a warm feeling, because, Pennsylvanian though these people might be, what they reminded her of the most was Arkansas, of a gun-toting, right-leaning, Christian, rural breed that she'd avoided and lightly derided growing up, but that she realized now she'd missed. She'd drifted up to some guys at a table and explained what she wanted—home defense, etcetera—and they'd quite solicitously shown her the kind of handgun she needed and made sure she understood exactly how to use it. Despite the fact that the men had been lightly flirting, she'd had the feeling that she was in the hands of uncles or cousins who would let nothing bad happen to her. (She knew there was an Arkansas joke in there somewhere, but fuck it.) It was all the more poignant for the fact that they'd felt like uncles and cousins from whom she'd been long estranged, due to her own negligence. She'd had the urge to hang out longer—some of those vendors had some cool stuff, antiques and samurai swords and so on—but she had a long drive, so she'd taken her handgun back to the new house in Stroudsburg where she hadn't yet unpacked a single box, then dropped the car off at the rental place, then taken the bus back to her new home.

Every morning she rode her bike to the bus station and chained it there to be retrieved at night. The commute to Manhattan was a drag, but it was nice to be living in a detached house with a tree in the yard. And Stroudsburg, being a new place, still seemed a touch exotic, though that would surely change.

Stewart got some voice messages from his mom.

When she called now—even when Maggie called—he normally let it go straight to voicemail. It wasn't that he didn't want to hear their voices, he always listened to the messages right away. This time, when he began to play his mother's first message, he was especially glad he hadn't picked up and talked to her live. If he'd been near his phone when she'd started calling, he would have eventually answered just this once, because she'd called multiple times, re-dialing each time her message went too long and cut her off, and if Stewart had seen her calling over and over like that he would have assumed someone had died.

He was in the living room when he started to listen to the first message, sitting on the couch he rented. A few seconds into the message he hung up and went upstairs to the roof to start it over again.

She'd left five messages. He saved each one, though to save them was like storing salt in a wound. In her voice he could hear how she was struggling not to cry. There was something heroic about her effort, about how almost completely she succeeded.

She was trying to lay out for him the muddled complex of her feelings, as a mother, a woman, and a citizen, about what had happened to Kevin, about having a son who'd been shot by his would-be victim.

This was the first time Stewart realized for sure that his mother had been more or less convinced by Jean's version of things, though he'd suspected as much before, with horror.

She told him that she knew his going to New York had something to do with Kevin. This was a testament to her motherly perception, since as far as Stewart knew she had no idea Jean was in New York, and so the link between Kevin and New York must have appeared opaque.

Since it was hard to figure out a way to say simultaneously all the contradictory things she wanted to express, she kept calling back and starting over, trying again.

Stewart listened to all her messages. Then he went back inside, because the open windows of his neighbors looked out onto this roof, whereas his roommates were gone. He curled up on the couch with his face against the back cushions and wept. Before long his roommates returned home. Stewart tried to hold himself still so that it would look like he was in a deep sleep, but no matter how tightly he clenched his body it still quivered and shook, and every once in a while his roommates heard him gasp out a sob, though he tried to muffle it. They pretended not to hear.

The next morning he went dutifully to Temple. He'd thought about calling in sick, but he was broke and Peter seemed to think Dan really might fire him if he did that again anytime soon. As he was leaving to go sit out his lunch hour in Bryant Park, he met Jean on the sidewalk. She'd been about to enter the bookstore.

They hadn't spoken since that exchange when she'd said "Hey" to him. Stewart would have continued walking, but her face gave him pause. She was looking at him as if he'd just said something she hadn't been able to make out.

He looked back at her and waited.

She stared at him a while, then said, "Hey."

This time, he only said, "Hey," in response.

She continued to study him. She said, "Are you finished with your work?"

"No. Lunch break."

"Oh. Yeah, me too. I was thinking about going in and browsing through the books, but...." She let the thought trail off.

Stewart waited for her to finish, then shrugged.

"Are you eating in the park?" she asked him.

"Just going over there to sit.... I don't have money to eat till payday tomorrow." He said this last bit accusingly, as if it were Jean's fault, then immediately felt embarrassed.

She was embarrassed, too. "Oh," she said. Then: "You know, I could buy you lunch."

"No."

"Come on. You can't go hungry."

"You know I can't let you."

That was true.... They were just standing there. The sidewalk was busy, people bustled past them. Stewart was about to go, when Jean said, "You know, I moved. To Stroudsburg."

Though he'd already taken a first step away, he waited. When she didn't say any more, he got impatient: "Okay. And?"

"I moved because I was scared. Of you." She said it like she regretted having to embarrass him.

It felt to Stewart like the whole universe was an elevator plummeting out of control. Ears ringing, he said, "I never said I was going to hurt you."

Jean shrugged. "Yeah. Well."

Now his face burned red, and he dropped his eyes. "I was never going to hurt you," he said. "It was stupid to move."

"How am I supposed to know?"

Instead of responding he walked across the street to the park.

From inside the store, from his high vantage behind the register, Charles had watched the whole exchange through the glass front doors. Once Stewart left, Jean just stood there for a moment on the sidewalk outside the doors. Then she finally walked into the store, but after hovering near the entrance a few seconds she turned and walked out, without looking at even one book. This all struck Charles as very suspicious, though he wasn't sure how to interpret any of it.

Once Stewart returned from his lunch break Charles waited for a chance to talk to him, but it was hard because Peter kept him on the register while he had Stewart stocking and straightening the shelves. Charles really wanted to go straight home after his shift (his roommates were both supposed to be gone, and there wasn't much he could do outside his apartment without spending money), but if there turned out to be no other chance to talk to Stewart, he would make time for it after work. It seemed important enough, even though Charles wasn't exactly best friends with the guy.

Fortunately, they both got sent to the basement and assigned to peeling the price stickers off books that were being returned to the publisher. The perfect set-up: just the two of them, sitting at a table a bit outside the empty break-room, slowly going through massive piles of unwanted books.

As usual, Stewart was distant and sullen. As an experiment, Charles waited to see if Stewart would address a word to him first. Of course he didn't; he never opened the conversation. Charles said, "So. I noticed you talking to that girl earlier, out front."

Stewart continued to peel stickers with the peeling tool, a flat dull blade. He gave so convincing an impression of not having heard him that Charles nearly repeated himself, which would have been stupid since Stewart was sitting there a foot away, and obviously *had* heard him. Charles said, "Are you and her, like, friends, now?"

This time Stewart did acknowledge what Charles had said, stopping his peeling and looking up at Charles like he was an idiot. "Are you kidding?"

"I only asked because it seemed like you were on friendly terms with her, is all."

Stewart didn't deign to answer. He tightened his lips and his jaw and returned to peeling.

Even though it seemed like Stewart might really flip out if Charles kept pressing, he would have felt irresponsible if he had let it go, after what Marissa had told him. "What did she talk to you about?"

It seemed like Stewart was going to keep peeling and not answer. At last, though, he said, "She told me she moved to Stroudsburg."

Charles's hands stopped peeling. He gaped at Stewart until Stewart blinked up at him, uncertainly. "What?" demanded Stewart.

"She told you about the Stroudsburg thing? Did she tell you exactly where?"

"Wait. 'The Stroudsburg thing'? How do *you* know she's moving to Stroudsburg?"

"Listen, man." For a moment Charles wondered if the words were going to come out, or if he was going to wind up only sitting there with his mouth open. "I know this is going to sound a little insane. But I have a friend who thinks Jean may be trying to, uh, set you up."

"*What?* What the fuck are you talking about?"

"It's nothing certain. It's just, you know, worth taking into consideration."

"What is? What friend?"

"She just thinks that maybe Jean is—"

"Who? Who are we talking about? Someone who you told about my brother?"

"No," Charles hurriedly assured him. Realizing that Stewart wasn't going to let him progress till he'd given some hint where he'd gotten his information, Charles gave up and said, "I've kind of been dating that redheaded girl who's friends with Jean. The one who came and yelled at you that one time."

The look Stewart gave Charles was a once-in-a-lifetime thing.

Charles kept going, hoping to be able to avoid having to explain in detail how that liaison had come about: "Marissa— that's the redhead—she says that Jean's got a gun in her new place in Stroudsburg, and she's planning to let you know where she lives now. Sort of like she did today. That way, if you do turn out to be … you know … and you go up to Stroudsburg and sort of, uh, go after her, then she'll be able to, uh...." Charles's pause this time was longer, and he had to drop his eyes before he could finish. "She'll be able to shoot you. In, like, self-defense. And because it'll be in Stroudsburg, she won't get in any trouble for having a gun."

Once done, Charles waited for what Stewart would do. He waited with both fascination and fear, though he couldn't have said what he was scared of. Maybe of Stewart punching him, or crying.

For now, Stewart was staring at him, his eyes so wide and the facial muscles around them so flexed it looked like it must hurt, his breathing coming in and going out like a bellows. "Jean said all that? That she was actually planning it?"

"Well. Marissa says she did. Basically."

"In other words, she's confirming everything I ever said about her. Right? About how she overreacts?"

"Uh. Well, I don't know, dude. What you're doing could legitimately freak someone out...."

"What the fuck is it I'm doing?!" said Stewart, nearly shouting. Charles drew back, wondering if that punch in the face was coming now. "I can't fucking move to New York like everybody else?! I can't work in a bookstore?! I can't sit down face-to-face just one time with the woman who shot my own brother for no good reason? Who made people think he was just some piece-of-shit rapist? Who made his own mother think that? Who made even me think that, sometimes?!"

"Hey!" Both Stewart and Charles jumped at Dan's shout, Charles so dramatically that his stool wobbled and he nearly fell off. Dan advanced on them, hands on his hips, white T-shirt tucked into blue shorts, five and a half wiry feet of humming indignation. "What the hell is going on here?!"

Charles gritted his teeth and fought the childish urge to object that he hadn't done anything, furious with Stewart for having gotten him in trouble with the boss and momentarily regretful for having mentioned any of this in the first place.

Charles decided to let Stewart field Dan's wrath, since he was the one who'd caused it, then immediately regretted that, too, when Stewart sullenly said, "We were just talking."

"You were just *yelling*! I could hear you all the way upstairs!" This seemed directed at both of them, and again Charles had to stop himself from pointing out woundedly that it was only Stewart he'd been able to hear. "Now cut that shit out and get back to work!"

Dan stalked back upstairs. Charles had been hoping he'd separate himself and Stewart, like a couple of quarreling kids. He didn't relish being down here with the guy, not while he was mad and while it was only a matter of time before he started demanding to know how much Charles and Marissa had been saying behind his back, how detailed their gossip had been. Of course, Charles could always lie and deny having revealed Stewart's version of things.

Stewart didn't seem interested in talking, though. He went back to peeling stickers, doing it so violently that he scratched and dented the covers.

"Hey, man," ventured Charles. "You're damaging the covers."

Stewart ignored him.

"Stewart, if Dan comes down here and sees that the books are all fucked up and he can't return them anymore, he's really going to lose his shit. At both of us."

Still Stewart continued to peel roughly, till he flung down his peeling tool and said, "Fuck this, I feel sick, I'm going home." He got up from his stool and began to walk around the table towards the stairs.

"Stewart!" said Charles, and reached out to stop him, but yanked his hand back before making contact. What did stop Stewart was affrontedness at the fact that Charles had been about to touch him, and he stared down at him with that wide-eyed glare he had. It made Charles nervous. But he forced himself to maintain eye contact. Trying for a soothing tone, he said, "Dude. You need this job, right? Because I think Dan is really going to fire you if you go home sick again. Especially right now while he's so pissed at you for yelling."

Stewart continued to glare at him, his chest rising and falling rapidly.

"Just ride it out, man," Charles pleaded. "You know?"

Stewart stared at him some more. Finally he muttered, "I got to take a shit," and walked to the employees' bathroom by the foot of the stairs.

Charles felt his tightened muscles disengaging somewhat. For once, he didn't mind being left alone with all the work. He went back to peeling, trying to move as fast as he could without damaging the books—the sooner this task was finished, the sooner he could escape from this underground chamber where he was shut in with this maniac.

He peeled like the wind, amazing himself. Meanwhile Stewart stayed locked in the toilet. Three times, employees came down, tried the door, and when they found it was locked rolled their eyes and headed back upstairs to the customers' bathroom— no one realized it was the same guy in there for an hour.

Dan came back downstairs. "Where's the other guy?" he demanded, hands on hips.

Charles timidly nodded towards the toilet and said, "In there." Dan followed his gaze with gradually relaxing suspicion, and muttered, "Well, okay."

Dan turned his attention to the books being prepped for return and was basically satisfied—there were only eleven left to do. So great had been Charles's desire to get out of there, he'd done the work of two people.

Eleven

Jean could tell that living in Stroudsburg might eventually start sucking, but for now it had the usual charm of a big change. She really did have a little front yard, and a little back yard too. In the front yard, a little tree. She didn't see herself here in ten years, but for now it was cute. The commute was a motherfucker, but even that had a spice of adventure to it. Actually it was just the expense that she blanched at. Riding her bike through the unbusy leafy streets to the bus station was a nice way to start the day. There was the gun, loaded, in the drawer of her bedside table. Once in a while she would remember it like an embarrassing afterthought. Sometimes it seemed to her that the gun was something which had been included with the house, that had been there when she'd arrived, and she had trouble remembering that the whole move had originally been for its sake.

The Monday when she told Stewart she'd moved to Stroudsburg, that was her one-week anniversary of doing the new commute. She'd moved her stuff in on the Sunday before. Or, well, she'd paid movers to move it for her, obviously. She thought of Stewart, with nothing but his rented couch in an apartment of strangers and his ten-dollars-an-hour job.

Stewart had never told her he was just renting a couch—the way she knew was through Penny. Penny had made friends with a woman named Maggie who worked in Little Rock's very last independent bookstore. It was in Hillcrest, where Penny liked to hang out, mulling through the frou-frou shops and corny little galleries. The women had been chatting about bookstores, and Maggie had said she had a friend working in a bookstore in New York, and Penny had said she had a friend up in New York, too, and within a few minutes Maggie had realized Penny was talking about Jean, and Penny had realized Maggie was talking about Stewart.

Immediately Maggie had gotten emotional. She'd poured forth to Penny everything she knew about Stewart's living conditions and his strange, formless quest. She was scared to think what might happen to him, going crazy all alone up there.

Penny had immediately reported everything she'd learned over the phone to Jean. As she'd listened, Jean had wondered if Maggie had wished she could ask Jean to look after Stewart. That would have been ridiculous, of course. How much of what Maggie had told Penny had been intended to get back to Jean and evoke some sympathy? Not in a cynical way, necessarily. It did sound like the guy could use sympathy. Jean would be a bizarre candidate for giving it to him, but then again it didn't sound like he really knew anyone else in town.

Now, Monday night, Jean was at her new home. It was quiet. Despite the commute, she still had some time before bed. She lounged in her chair, a book in her hand, listening to the silence of the house and the whoosh of traffic on the busy street many blocks away.

Not much furniture. If she stayed in this small house she'd have to fill it. The cutest piece was her nightstand table. She'd gone out shopping for one so as to have someplace to keep the gun, though when she'd found it, it had been so cute that she'd forgotten about its purpose.

She sat with the book dangling from her hand as night fell outside. She thought about pouring herself a glass of wine but couldn't be bothered. She was feeling too lazy and cozy even to put the book down. Before long it would probably slip from her fingers and tumble to the floor.

Maybe, after all, it was nice to be someplace a little peaceful.

Idly she let her gaze crawl towards the window. What an exotic luxury, having a window so close to the ground, yet that didn't open onto a busy noisy street. Instead it opened onto the quiet of her yard.

It was night and she had the light on inside, so it was hard to see out. But it looked to her like there was maybe something in the window.

Her book dropped and she scrambled out of her chair, hearing a strange little noise issue from her throat. There was a guy out there!

She backed up and braced her feet upon the floor and for some reason pointed down at it. "Who's there?!" she demanded, and "Go away!"

There definitely was a human head in the gloom beyond her windowpane. Now it darted off. With horror Jean realized it had gone in the direction of her front door. She raced for it, flinging herself against it as the person outside pounded on it with his fist, so that she felt the shockwaves of it vibrate through her body. But the door was already locked, naturally.

"Go away!" she said again. Then she had a moment of crazy embarrassment: what if it was only someone knocking? What if she'd imagined the man outside, and was putting on the mental breakdown show for someone who'd brought cookies to welcome her to the neighborhood?

It wasn't a regular knock, though. And now she heard Stewart's voice, saying, "Let me in, I only want to have a conversation!," even as he pounded on the door like what he only wanted was to beat her into a bag of jelly.

"Fuck you!" Jean was angry to hear how scared she sounded. She asked herself suddenly what she was doing leaning against the door like this, letting it vibrate her as that maniac outside hit it. She jumped up and backed away from it a few feet. Then she stood her ground and shouted, "Go away, I said!"

"Why should I?" he shouted through the door. "I only want to have a conversation!"

"Go away!"

"Just talk to me, you crybaby chickenshit!"

"I have a gun!" she yelled, startling herself by remembering it.

"So fucking shoot me with it!"

There was nothing else for it. Jean marched back to her bedroom. Because the house was still new to her, she opened the door to the hall closet first instead. That made for a nightmarishly disorienting second or two. She marched back to the front door, the cold gun hanging from her arm like it would drag her shoulder from its socket. "I've got this fucking gun right now to shoot you with it!"

"Good!"

At a loss, she stared at the door. The gun was impossibly heavy, like it was being acted upon by the gravity of some other, bigger planet. Jean raised it and pointed the barrel in the general direction of the door. Maybe he would eventually break it down, and then she would shoot him.

A wave of disgust, horror, and preemptive guilt washed through her. There were other options than that! She had a hard time even pointing the barrel at the area of the door she guessed he was behind.

That she should call 911 was a no-brainer. But it was so sad and pathetic, the notion of him being handcuffed and taken to jail, him with no friends to come and see him; the notion of his parents way down in Conway getting the call that their only living son was in jail, of their going to the Wal-Mart SuperCenter in the middle of the night to FedEx the bail money. If only she could simply find some way to make him go away.

She remembered her back door. Leaving him to continue his banging at the front of the house, she hurried to the back. She opened that door and leaned out into her yard, lit by the uncanny ambient street lights. She took a deep breath, but the words hitched to a stop in her throat; this was the first time she'd ever tried to scream in public, and she found herself with a strong inhibition against it. But she forced herself to suck in a second breath, then shout as loud as she could, "Help!"

The pounding on the front door stopped. She slammed and locked the back door again, in case he was running around to the back of the house to shut her up.

Jean stood well away from the back door, watching it like it might attack, her gun half-raised.

Nothing. No noise from the door. Nothing from the front, either. Maybe he was lurking, waiting for her to poke her head out so he could attack her. Again, the sensible thing was to call the police. Also the moral thing, if she really thought the alternative might be to blow Stewart's brains out. The truth was that her blood was up and she didn't want to be some fucking damsel. She was mad enough to want to fight this out, one-on-one.

She waited for some sign of him, till it was clear she would either have to call the police after all, or go look around outside to see if he was still there. She decided to do the stupid thing and go outside herself.

Gripping her gun, she went back to the front door, unlocked it, and then, when no one slammed themselves against it to force it open, she very slowly stuck her head out, bringing her gun hand out at the same time. She was squeezing the gun so tight, and her body was quivering with such tension, that it was just luck she didn't inadvertently pull the trigger.

Stewart was out there in the middle of the road, stepping back and forth uncertainly. As she stuck her head out and looked at him, he stopped taking steps and shoved his hands into his pockets, as if he knew he looked like an idiot but there was nothing he could do about it anymore.

"What're you doing out there, asshole?" she called.

"I took off running when you started yelling," he called back. "But then you stopped. So I was waiting around to see if you were going to start up again."

"Okay."

Instead of standing still in the middle of the street, he was now walking towards her, hands still jammed in his pockets. He wasn't hurrying; it looked almost like a stroll. Nevertheless: "I have a gun," Jean warned.

"I'm not going to hurt you," he said, scornfully, as if the very idea were typical of her suspicious mind, and he hadn't done anything to justify her alarm.

Just like your brother, she considered saying; but she didn't say it, and afterwards was glad she hadn't.

Instead, she only said, "Whatever. If you move towards me fast, I'll shoot you."

He didn't respond at all, just walked off the street across her yard, then sat on the end of her porch, a few feet away from where she hovered at the front door with the gun. His back was three-quarters to her. He took his hands from his pockets and began compulsively rubbing his palms on his jeans. Jean kept the gun almost but not quite pointed at him. She wondered if, assuming she did wind up shooting him, the fact that she'd let him sit on her porch first would compromise her legally.

They just stayed like that without speaking. Jean stared at Stewart, but he seemed unable to look at her.

"So what the fuck are you doing?" she finally demanded.

"What the fuck are *you* doing?"

"Sitting at home. Where I live. Which is miles and miles from where *you* live. So: what are you doing here?"

He didn't answer. He gritted his teeth and scowled out into the night. After a moment, he said, "It's weird that no one came when you yelled for help."

Jean had been thinking the same thing. "I know," she said. The two of them gazed at the sealed houses, many of which still had lights on inside, and they silently commiserated together over the inhumanity of her neighbors.

Jean pulled the conversation back to his invasion of her home: "So what are you doing here? I moved to Stroudsburg to get away from you, no offense."

"That's not what I heard."

"What the fuck does that mean?"

He told her how Charles had warned him that she was moving to Pennsylvania so that she could tell Stewart where she lived, and so that she'd be able to shoot him if and when he came looking for her. He had no reservations about letting her know that he'd gotten his info from Charles, who'd gotten it from Marissa (though Stewart didn't remember her name, and just called her the redhead).

Jean listened with mounting outrage to the spin Marissa had put on her motives. "But you obviously didn't believe them," she said. "If you really thought the whole point of me moving out here was to kill you, you would have stayed away. Yet here you are."

Stewart only smirked into the distance. Jean made a note to try to figure out what that smirk meant before letting him go. For now, she said, "How did you know where I was?"

"I trolled around on your Facebook page till I found your roommate's name. Then I got her number from Information. I called her and said I was your cousin and that I needed your new mailing address so that we could have flowers delivered to you, and that I couldn't ask you because it was supposed to be a surprise."

"That fucking bitch. I explicitly asked her not to give out my new address."

"No, I was really convincing. I told her we were sending the flowers for the fifteenth anniversary of some award you won in the seventh grade. It was so specific and weird, it had to be true."

For a second Jean wondered how he knew exactly how long ago she'd been in the seventh grade. But of course he remembered her age relative to Kevin's. He would have learned that at the time of the shooting. "I knew I shouldn't have told her the address here," she said.

Stewart stared straight ahead.

She sat there looking at his profile. Her gun hand had relaxed unconsciously. She was less wary now and to an observer would have simply seemed absorbed, as she tried to figure this guy out. She even sat on the porch as well, there in her doorway.

She said again, "But you must not have thought I moved up here and bought a gun for the sole purpose of luring you here and killing you. Because in that case you wouldn't have come."

At first Stewart didn't say anything. There was only that smirk again.

After a few seconds he said, "If you'd shot me through that door when I wasn't even breaking in, just because I was knocking hard, then everyone would know you were an overreacting fraidy-cat, just like I always said you were."

"So, what? You're willing to get yourself shot and killed, and set me up to do it, just to prove you were right and I was wrong? What good'll it do you to be right, afterwards? You want to be dead that bad?"

Once more she thought he wasn't going to answer, except that his smirk got deeper, like he might actually laugh. Finally he said, "Whatever."

Jean started crying. "Kevin just really scared me that time, Stewart. He just really scared me."

Stewart was crying, too. "He wasn't going to hurt you."

"I really think he was." For some reason she had scooted closer to Stewart and was leaning towards him, like she was going to touch him.

"No," he said. "No." He rose to his feet. Jean kept her eyes on him, almost hungrily. Whereas she let the tears run freely down her face, he hid his with his hand, and tried to wipe them away as if he thought he could keep anyone from finding out about them. "It's not your fault," he said. "I just wish I'd...." He trailed off.

They were both there crying on her new suburban porch, her looking at him and him averting his eyes.

"I have to go," he said, turning his body away from the house.

"Do you need a ride to the bus stop?" she said. It came out almost a wail. She didn't even have a car. Maybe she was thinking of calling him a cab.

"No," he said. "No, I should go. I wish I hadn't come." He left her yard and staggered down the road in the direction of the bus station. Was there even a night bus? Jean watched him go. Even after he was out of sight she sat a while and wept.

Twelve

Charles called Marissa several times and left voice messages. He tried not to call *too* often, and if she'd never returned his calls he would have given up, albeit regretfully. But she did return them, with cheerful voice messages, or with texts in which she included lots of x's and o's, and in which she apologized for being so busy and promised they'd get together soon. So Charles held out hope. But he was savvy enough to know, as two weeks stretched into a third, that his chances were stretching thinner, too. Not a lot he could do about it. When entering or leaving the bookstore he kept an eye out, and it would have been nice to bump into her and start re-charming her. But it would be counter-productive if he started hovering outside the building, lying creepily in wait.

Just when he was about to once and for all switch the primary focus of his financial and masturbatory energy to some other girl, she called and said they should set up a date.

"How about Mexican?" she suggested, when he asked where she would like to meet. He was happy to agree. In terms of getting drunk and gorged for a halfway-reasonable cost, at a halfway-decent place, Mexican was probably the best bet.

She picked the place. It was a spot near her in Brooklyn. If it had been in Queens instead he would have worried less about the price—some of those uppity Brooklyn restaurants were as pricey as Manhattan's. On the other hand, there was a chance she wanted to meet near her apartment because she was considering having him come over afterwards.

They kissed hello, only a peck but on the lips. They got their margaritas, they got their chips and salsa. Marissa briskly flattened a napkin across her lap; it gave the impression that she was settling in and getting down to business. "So," she said. "Want to do the post-op on Stewart and Jean?"

The drama between Jean and Stewart had been a huge boon when he'd needed some reason to talk to Marissa, and it wasn't like he wasn't still fascinated by it. But he wanted to progress, to be able to talk with her about her life, about his own. "Sure," he said, dipping a chip in the salsa and eating it. Because he was with a woman he was hoping to seduce, he didn't load the chip with as much salsa as he would have done normally, and he was more careful than usual not to let the sauce dribble down his chin. "But I haven't been around him all that much. Actually been trying to get a different job."

"Oh yeah? Where?"

"I want to get on as a tutor at Kaplan, tutoring kids to take the SAT."

"Oh yeah? That's cool."

"It's kind of a scam. I mean, not Kaplan, they're legit, I think. But the SAT's and all those standardized tests like that, they're kind of bullshit. You don't have to actually know anything. You just have to know how to work the test."

"Well. You have to know how to read."

"Okay. That's true. The SAT does test for basic literacy, yes." They munched and drank for a bit. Charles said, "How's *your* job?"

"It's been a little weird and stressful. Jean got mad for some reason and decided to quit talking to me."

"Oh. Yeah?"

"I think she thinks I kind of breached her privacy with that stuff I told you, about the gun, and Stroudsburg."

Charles wondered if the implication was that it was his fault she'd found out Marissa had spilled the beans, because he'd told Stewart and it had somehow worked its way back to Jean through him. But Marissa showed no sign of wanting to pursue that line of blame. She just talked about how Jean had asked Marissa if she'd told anyone about what they'd discussed that day at Chevy's, and how ever since she'd seemed, if not cold, then uninterested in communicating about anything unrelated to work.

"How about Stewart?" asked Marissa.

"Same here. Like I said, I don't really hang out with him all that much anymore." Charles frowned. "But so, how did Jean find out you were telling people about the Stroudsburg gun thing?"

She looked up at him from under her brows. "You didn't tell her?"

"Tell *Jean*? No. I've never talked to her."

"You didn't tell anyone else?"

"Well, I mean, I told Stewart. Like we, I mean, we *said* I was going to tell him, I thought that was the whole point of you telling me about it in the first place. About what you thought was going on, and all that. Did you tell anyone besides me?"

"No."

On the one hand, Charles figured that was a good sign, if true—maybe he was her main confidante. On the other, he worried this might mean she was holding him responsible for the leak.

It sounded like the only other possibility was Stewart.

He made a face. "I mean, like I said, I told Stewart. Do you think Stewart would have talked about it with Jean?"

She frowned and double-dipped a chip. "Maybe," she said. "But that would be weird. Although, I don't know—their whole thing is pretty weird."

Charles was silent a moment, wondering what had happened between Stewart and Jean. Between Kevin and Jean, for that matter. He supposed no one would ever know for sure.

The food came. Charles managed to change the subject to Marissa's work. They talked about that a while. Then Charles told, in a breezy natural way, some stories he'd prepared. Marissa laughed at them, in the right places. But when he reached for her hand on the table, she gently and discreetly withdrew it.

And when the check came, no matter how he fought for the right to pay, she insisted on going dutch.

Outside, Charles stood looking at her, trying not to be too yearning about it, as she lit a cigarette. Once she had it lit, she smiled at him. The smile was restrained. "So," she said. "I live over this way." She pointed behind herself. "But your train is this way?" She pointed straight ahead.

Charles shrugged in vague, unwilling agreement. "You feel like getting a coffee or something?" he asked.

She grimaced. "Ah, then I'd never get to sleep. You know?"

"So maybe a beer?"

"I better not. That margarita knocked me out."

"Okay. Well. It was good seeing you!"

"You, too!"

"Let's do this again soon."

"Totally."

He went to hug her. She let him. But when he put his face near hers she drew it back. In a mildly apologetic tone she said, "Hey, what if we didn't kiss this time?"

She said, "Or we could just kiss on the cheeks. How's that? We'll kiss on the cheeks, like friends." And she kissed him on his cheek, then drew her head back to check his reaction.

"Oh well, it's non-optimal, but hey," he said, and pretended to laugh.

Marissa pretended to believe he was really laughing, and to laugh along with him. He let her go.

He watched her walk away, feeling dense, sad, and sodden. Felt so bad he laughed at himself, silently. Made himself turn away, start walking towards the subway station. He wished he'd gotten the chance to fuck that hot skinny angular redhead with the big wild eyes. It wasn't simply horniness, or the male desire to add another notch to his belt, though partly it was that. Mainly, it was that, if they'd fucked, that would have been a real, memorable experience they would definitely have shared. It would have sealed in those hours they'd spent together, and insured their continued existence. Now, they were likely to just forget each other. If he bumped into her at a party in seven years or whatever, there would be no proof they'd ever really known each other at all.

As the years passed, Jean and Stewart would see each other occasionally, by chance, in passing, on the street, at a movie. Sometimes they would say hello, sometimes they'd each pretend not to have seen the other and would keep walking, not out of hard feelings but simply because they were both in a hurry. Once they bumped into each other back in Arkansas, when they were both there for a visit. But that was years into the future.

The first time they saw each other again, after the thing at Jean's place in Stroudsburg, was at the Hungarian Pastry Shop. Jean's year-long Pennsylvania adventure had ended and she'd recently moved back to New York. That year of spending nearly a third of her waking life commuting had felt almost like a monastic withdrawal, and it was disorienting to be back in the city full-time. She had decided to start keeping a journal. She'd bought a nice one, with faux-leather binding and faux-handmade paper, and now she was sitting at one of the tables at the Hungarian, coffee in hand, looking at her crisp blank new journal and ready to get started. Some guy who was returning to his table, having gone to the front to get a refill, did a double-take as he was walking by and stopped. Jean looked up. It was Stewart.

She didn't invite him to sit down, but he stood next to her table and they chatted for a few minutes.

She asked if he was still at Temple. "Oh, no," he said. The place had been nice, but he'd managed to piss Dan off often enough that he'd decided he should go ahead and quit before he got fired. Right now he was working at Barnes and Noble, which sucked because it was barely enough to pay his rent (he'd moved into a place with some people, he had his own room now). He'd put in to become a guard at the Metropolitan Museum. He figured that would be an okay life, standing around looking at the art. And it had health insurance and was union. Meanwhile he was toying with the idea of trying to become a receptionist at a yoga studio. He thought maybe he'd like to try yoga, and figured this would be a way to get free lessons.

Jean was still at the same company. But their office had moved downtown. That was why she hadn't been to Temple in a while. Now she sometimes spent her lunch hour browsing in a different bookstore, the smaller McNally-Jackson. But that was less convenient to her new workplace than Temple had been, so she didn't go to bookstores as often anymore.

Before Stewart went back to his own table, Jean burst into laughter. Smiling, a little tightly, Stewart watched her laugh. "What's up?" he asked.

"I was just remembering our date, and how it blew my mind when I found out you were from Arkansas," she said. "I mean, it just blew my fucking mind."

They each worked at their own table—Jean wrote in her journal; she didn't know what Stewart was writing. His table was in the back, and hers was near the front, facing away from him. When she got up to leave she glanced his way. He was hunched over, writing something, working intensely. She thought about going back to say goodbye to him, but they'd already said whatever they were going to say, so she just left.

If you enjoyed this book, please help spread the word about it; take a moment to leave a review on Goodreads, Amazon, or any other online forum.

And please sign up for our mailing list, at saltimbanquebooks.com

ABOUT THE AUTHOR

J. Boyett is a novelist, playwright, filmmaker, and founder of Saltimbanque Books, and can be reached at jboyettjboyett@gmail.com.

For more information check out jboyett.net.

ALSO FROM SALTIMBANQUE BOOKS:

THE LITTLE MERMAID: A HORROR STORY, by J. Boyett

Brenna has an idyllic life with her heroic, dashing, lifeguard boyfriend Mark. She knows it's only natural that other girls should have crushes on the guy. But there's something different about the young girl he's rescued, who seemed to appear in the sea out of nowhere—a young girl with strange powers, who will stop at nothing to have Mark for herself.

BENJAMIN GOLDEN DEVILHORNS, by Doug Shields

A collection of stories set in a bizarre universe: the lord of cockroaches breathes the same air as a genius teenage girl with a thing for criminals, a ruthless meat tycoon who hasn't figured out that secret gay affairs are best conducted out of town, and a telepathic mind-controlling bowling ball. Yes, the bowling ball breathes.

RICKY, by J. Boyett

Ricky's hoping to begin a new life upon his release from prison; but on his second day out, someone murders his sister. Determined to find her killer, but with no idea how to go about it, Ricky follows a dangerous path, led by clues that may only be in his mind.

BROTHEL, by J. Boyett

What to do for kicks if you live in a sleepy college town, and all you need to pass your courses is basic literacy? Well, you could keep up with all the popular TV shows. Or see how much alcohol you can drink without dying. Or spice things up with the occasional hump behind the bushes. And if that's not enough you could start a business....

THE VICTIM (AND OTHER SHORT PLAYS), by J. Boyett

In The Victim, April wants Grace to help her prosecute
the guys who raped them years before. The only problem
is, Grace doesn't remember things that way.... Also
included:
A young man picks up a strange woman in a bar, only to
realize she's no stranger after all;
An uptight socialite learns some outrageous truths about
her family;
A sister stumbles upon her brother's bizarre sexual rite;
A first date ends in grotesque revelations;
A love potion proves all too effective;
A lesbian wedding is complicated when it turns out one
bride's brother used to date the other bride.

COMING IN 2016:

COLD PLATE SPECIAL, by Rob Widdicombe

Jarvis Henders has finally hit the beige bottom of his beige life, his law-school dreams in shambles, and every bar singing to him to end his latest streak of sobriety. Instead of falling back off the wagon, he decides to go take his life back from the child molester who stole it. But his journey through the looking glass turns into an adventure where he's too busy trying to guess what will come at him next, to dwell on the ghosts of his past.

I'M YOUR MAN, by F. Sykes

It's New York in the 1990's, and every week for years Fred has cruised Port Authority for hustlers, living a double life, dreaming of the one perfect boy that he can really love. When he meets Adam, he wonders if he's found that perfect boy after all ... and even though Adam proves to be very imperfect, and very real, Fred's dream is strengthened to the point that he finds it difficult to awake.

THE UNKILLABLES, by J. Boyett

Gash-Eye already thought life was hard, as the Neanderthal slave to a band of Cro-Magnons. Then zombies attacked, wiping out nearly everyone she knows and separating her from the Jaw, her half-breed son. Now she fights to keep the last remnants of her former captors alive. Meanwhile, the Jaw and his father try to survive as they maneuver the zombie-infested landscape alongside time-travelers from thirty thousand years in the future.... Destined to become a classic in the literature of Zombies vs. Cavemen.

Made in the USA
Columbia, SC
21 November 2021

49004713R00065